Madrugada

A CYCLE OF EROTIC FICTIONS

First Edition

Published by The Nazca Plains Corporation
Las Vegas, Nevada
2009

ISBN: 978-1-934625-97-2

Published by

The Nazca Plains Corporation ®
4640 Paradise Rd, Suite 141
Las Vegas NV 89109-8000

PUBLISHER'S NOTE
Madrugada is a work of fiction created wholly by *David May's* imagination. All characters are fictional and any resemblance to any persons living or deceased is purely by accident. No portion of this book reflects any real person or events.

Cover Photo, Vish Studio
Art Director, Blake Stephens

DEDICATION

We are, when in love, in an unnatural state.
- Proust

For Phil Cash who awakened a heart I thought dead and in so
doing, took on the awesome responsibility of loving me.

And in memory of David Lourea, who gave me Nachman and so
much more.

Madrugada (Portuguese): The time between midnight and dawn.

ACKNOWLEDGEMENTS

Something Akin to Love first appeared in an altered (read: censored) form in the July 1988 issue of *Honcho*.

Jason, Cat first appeared in a somewhat different version in *Drummer* #86 in 1985. Essentially the same version that appears here was also published in *Rogues of San Francisco*, GLB Press 1993, edited by Bill Lee; and in *Meltdown!*, Richard Kasak Books 1994, edited by Caro Soles.

Cutting Threads first appeared in a more verbose form in *Drummer* #75 in June 1984.

Tyke first appeared in a somewhat different, and more far-fetched, version in *Mach* #10 in 1986.

Officer Beltman first appeared in *Mach* #11 in 1986.

Unnatural Song first appeared in a slightly different form in the August 1986 issue of *Honcho*.

The Circle is Complete first appeared in *Drummer* #125 in 1989.

The Center of the Maze first appeared in *Drummer* #139 in 1990. It also appeared in *Rogues of San Francisco*, GLB Press 1993, edited by Bill Lee.

Thanks to all the editors I've worked with at the above anthologies and periodicals. Special thanks to Steven Saylor, who accepted my first story (**Cutting Threads**), and to my favorite editor at *Drummer*, the late Paul Martin Heltsley, who pushed me to do better.

This book was originally published in not quite the same form by BadBoy Books.

Madrugada

A CYCLE OF EROTIC FICTIONS

First Edition

David May

CONTENTS

AUTHORS NOTE

These stories were written between 1984 and 1995. They take place in a world not unlike our own between the late 1970s and the early 1990s. I had the idea of creating a cycle of stories with overlapping characters when the first two stories (**Cutting Threads** and **Jason, Cat**) were first published in *Drummer*. While the bars, clubs and street names mentioned in the stories are (or were) real places, the characters are completely fictitious and any resemblance to anyone living or dead is purely coincidental.

SOMETHING AKIN TO LOVE

When love flies it is remembered not as love but as something else.

- E.M. Forster

This is about Will.

His father called him Bill, his mother said William, and his brothers and sisters insisted on Billy. He called himself Will, and Jay called him Willy-Boy.

Will hated being called Willy-Boy.

He lived in the part of San Francisco called the Duboce Triangle with Jay, his lover. Jay was much older (somewhere in his forties, though his exact age kept shifting) than Will (who was in his early twenties). Jay owned the house they lived in and was quick to remind Will who the homeowner was whenever they got in a fight, and they fought often.

They fought with insinuations, barbed retorts and calculated cruelty. Then they'd fuck their brains out.

They had no friends, only tricks. There had been the pretense of fidelity at first, though Will always knew that Jay was fucking around. So Will fucked around too, stayed out as late as he wanted, and grew back the mustache he had shaved off because Jay hated facial hair. Jay fought it at first, but finally accepted it when Will caught him in one too many lies and said he'd leave Jay then and there.

It hadn't been a particularly important lie. Jay lied all the time – about his work, the price he paid for the house, his age, his ex-lovers and tricks, his family. Jay lied so often that Will wouldn't have known the truth if he'd heard it. But this lie was too stupid to tolerate. Jay said he'd been with his sister Janet all afternoon.

"Janet?"

"Yeah, Janet. I told you this morning that I was going to Marin to see her."

That was a lie because Jay was still asleep (or pretending to be asleep) when Will had gotten up to go to the gym. Later, Will had run into Janet at Macy's and had had lunch with her.

Will told Jay as much, and Jay said he was being spied on, and Will said that Jay was one sick queen, and Jay said Will could move out of Jay's house, and Will said he would. Then Jay said that they were arguing over nothing and that he had really been shopping for Will's birthday present ("at Gumps") which Will knew was a lie because the only birthday Jay ever remembered was his own. Will told Jay he could fuck himself, walked out and spent the night at the baths.

That was when the relationship became officially "open."

The years of Jay's lies, Will's retaliatory whoring, constant fighting, threats of violence, ultimatums, bitterness and reconciliations followed by furious fucking, continued.

Jay was content with their life, but Will's eyes wandered constantly. He saw lovers eating quietly together in restaurants and wondered why he wasn't one of them. He met handsome men who appreciated him and asked why he stayed with Jay. Will couldn't say why, though he knew he ought to leave.

Later on he'd understand that he stayed with Jay out of fear of the world. He had nowhere to go, no friends. The only life he knew was the guilty insanity of life with Jay. He had no sense of himself apart from the insanity, and so he stayed. But then things changed. Will met Aaron and discovered who he was. Considering the nature of his relationship with Jay, who he was shouldn't have surprised Will. But it did.

Being a Macy's queen, the first thing Will noticed about Aaron was Aaron's suit. It was a fine charcoal gray, full cut – nothing fanciful or Italian about it. A *man's* suit, Will thought, standing on the corner of Post and Kearney waiting for the light to change. The sort of suit Jay is too silly to wear, he thought.

Then he noticed Aaron, who had the build and handsome, square-jawed, bearded face to do the suit justice. Aaron had already noticed Will and nodded to him. Will nodded back.

"How are you today?"

"Okay," said Will.

Then the lights changed. Aaron said, "See you," and disappeared into the street.

Will was disappointed. He'd been certain they'd sit (or at least stand) together on the streetcar and talk; that Aaron would pursue him and that Will would be coy, giving Aaron his phone number only when pressed for it. He had expected to tell Aaron what he always told the men he met, since it was always true – "I have a lover" – before agreeing to get together the following evening. Will was hurt by Aaron's lack of cooperation.

That had been in the fall, and Will didn't see Aaron for months, though he thought about him now and then between tricks and fights with Jay, or when he was jerking-off.

The second time he saw Aaron was almost six months later. He was standing on Market Street waiting for the streetcar when Aaron walked by with another man. Will watched the two men and wondered if they were lovers. Aaron saw him and nodded again, this time raising his hand in a wave as well. Will returned the greeting, flattered to be remembered.

Will didn't notice Aaron's friend look back and ask who Will was, or hear Aaron answer, "Some kid who needs his ass whipped."

Will saw him a few more times downtown after that, and they always greeted each other, smiled and said hello. But Will never got to tell Aaron his name, let alone his phone number.

In June came the Parade. Will went with Jay, who made disparaging remarks about each group in the procession whether they were dykes, drag queens, niggers, gooks, spics, religious weirdoes, commies or perverts. All of which "gave gay a bad name."

Will, not happy to spend the day with Jay, got separated from him in the crowd. He cruised the men he wanted, snubbed the ones he didn't. Then he turned around and, like a dream, saw Aaron's friend Pete (the one from downtown) looking straight at him.

Will wasn't prepared for what he saw, for the hard edge that black leather gave Pete's bearded face. First Will saw the leather cap, then the chaps and boots. Looking for something familiar, Will admired the firm bare torso and chest etched with thick brown hair along the expanse of the pecs and coming to a fine point at the navel. Then he saw the two gold rings, one in each nipple, and the gold chain suspended between them.

Not quite sure of what he was doing, Will reached out and caressed the hairy chest, damp with sweat in the afternoon heat.

Will brought his fingers to his tongue to taste the sweat.

"You want something, kid?" asked Pete.

Will swallowed hard, and not knowing what to say, walked away. He heard someone laugh as he tried to lose himself in the crush of shirtless men.

"What did you want with him?" asked Jay, suddenly appearing from the crowd. "He's *weird*. Some kind of pervert!"

Unable to answer the same question twice in as many minutes, Will decided to find out what it was he wanted from Pete.

Will wasn't naive. He'd learned a few things about what he really liked; things Jay would never go along with: like getting his ass slapped when he got fucked, being held down, being Daddy's boy. He knew, in fact, that he liked sex to be, at the very least, rough and tumble. And being ordered about in public – and it would be hard to find a place more public than United Nations Plaza on Gay Freedom Day – after being ordered about by Jay all these years, seemed, if not the next logical step, not so far removed either.

He approached Pete.

"Sir?"

"Yeah, kid?"

"May I?" And he got down on his knees and licked Pete's boots as he'd seen another boy do in a bar once.

Pete pulled Will up off his knees, took his face in both hands and kissed him tenderly, deeply. Will's cock got hard and inched its way down the brief cut-off Levis he was wearing, an outfit Jay didn't approve saying it looked cheap and made "fags look bad."

Pete unlocked the dog collar strapped around his left boot and secured it around Will's neck. In return, Will kissed Pete's gloved hand and offered to lick the sweat off his chest and armpits.

"Not yet, boy," said Pete. "First finish licking my boots. Then we'll see about you earning my sweat."

Will obeyed at once. A few minutes later they rode to Pete's flat on Hattie Street. Still eager to lick the sweat off Pete's body, Will was told that he might yet earn that honor, but first Pete had to pee. Will stood where he was and waited for Pete to go to the toilet and return. Pete, on the other hand, undid his pants where he was and looked at Will expectantly.

"Boy, I said I have to pee."

Then Will understood. Pete held Will close, kissed him again, then forced him to his knees. Will opened his mouth for the stream of hot piss, trying hard to swallow it all, but spilling much of it.

"Look at that mess, fuck-up! You got it all over yourself. No sweat for you. And no dick and no cum."

Will hung his head to hide his shame. He was afraid that he might cry.

"Yes, sir. I'm sorry, sir."

Touched by this display of contrition, but not wanting to made a liar, Pete tied Will up and beat him with a heavy belt. Afterwards, he fucked Will and then, as a reward, let Will lick the sweat off his body.

After that, Will saw Pete once or twice a week. When he wasn't with Pete, Will explored Folsom Street, discovering in it things he'd only heard of before: the men, the bars, the sex clubs, the power. The men South of Market were so different from Jay. Will had stumbled onto another world and fell in love with it. He saw men coupling in cars, on their bikes, through their windows, on rooftops.

One night he caught himself saying out loud: "This is where I belong." The sound of his own voice startled Will. He looked around to see if anyone had heard him. The street was deserted, but Will felt that he'd been hard and accepted, as if the street had a soul of its own.

On another night, he saw Pete leaning against the bar of the Ramrod, talking with a friend. Will found a shadowed corner to sit in and stayed there to watch. As he watched men in the bar, he though to himself, I've found my home. As if in answer, Pete stood in front of him, collar in hand. Will knelt down on the floor and Pete secured the collar around his neck before leading him down Folsom Street on a leash.

"I never see you anymore," said Jay the next afternoon. Will had been out all night and most of that day. There was a bounce in his walk, the sort that comes only from a good beating. "Where do you go at night? What's his name?"

"Whose name?"

"The guys getting your ass when I'm not."

This was true. Will hadn't let Jay as much as touch him in over a month, even going so far as to sleep alone. He didn't answer.

"And another thing, you're dressing weird now. You've got that leather vest on all the time. And now you've got those boots, too. What's next? *Chaps?*"

Jay threw out the last word as if it were an insult. Will turned to face Jay.

"I got measured for my chaps this morning. *And* I just decided to have my tits pierced."

"You *are* getting weird!"

There was a pause as each waited for the other to back down. Will took off his vest.

"That's more like," said Jay, thinking he'd won.

Then Will undid his shirt and pants.

"Baby…" Jay whispered, thinking Will was undressing for sex.

Then Will dropped his jeans and turned around to show Jay the explosion of welts and bruises that covered his backside after a night with Pete. Until that moment, he'd been careful to hide any marks Pete left. Now he wore them with pride.

"Omigod!"

Will pus his clothes back on and faced Jay defiantly.

"Maybe you'd better find another place to live," said Jay pulling out his only card. "I'm not gonna live with a pervert."

"I already did," said Will. "I'm moving South of Market and getting away from you – *queen!*"

The next day Will moved with the help of his new friends, boys like himself that he'd met at the bars or through Pete. One of them, who wore a thick collar around his throat, had borrowed his master's truck to help Will move. There wasn't much to move, really, since most of what in the house belonged to Jay. When they were done, Will took his friends to Hamburger Mary's for dinner. They huddled together over the table and talked about the men they were seeing. Only Alan, who wore the collar, was owned outright. Will envied him.

Once Will had moved, he spent each night in his leather, walking the dimly lit streets. He felt embraced in the darkness. And it occurred to him, as he stepped over the slumped figure of a sleeping drunk on the sidewalk, that he was most at home in the darkness, in a world far removed from the safety of his family's suburbia or the middle-class affections of living with Jay. Not being analytical, he never stopped to think about what this might mean, or of the nature of the path he had chosen. He'd been accepted into this world. For the first time in his life, he had friends with whom he felt close. He felt loved. He was safe, and that was enough.

"It's Folsom, you know?" he told his friends as they sat together on the steps of a warehouse one warm afternoon. "At night, especially. I can walk around for hours and almost taste it, even feel it in the air."

No one asked him what he felt in the darkness of the alleys. They only nodded their ascent.

"You, too?" Jim asked.

That was the only comment, because none else was needed. Will felt more at home than ever.

One night Pete invited Will to a party. "A play party," he said. "Wear a pair of jeans you don't care about and your boots. Nothing else."

"It's winter, sir. May I wear a jacket?

"I'll think about it."

On the night of the party, Will met Pete in front of the Eagle. As ordered, Will was kneeling in front of the entrance, head bowed, his hands behind his back as if bound. He waited at the assigned time until Pete showed up an hour later. A collar and leash were attached to Phil's neck. Without a word, he was led into a waiting cab.

The Catacombs was on the edge of the warehouse district on Shotwell Street, surrounded by a neighborhood that even Will, with his affinity for dark alleys, wouldn't walk through at night. Once inside, Will was blindfolded, tied up and put in a cage where he was left for the rest of the night. Will heard cries of anguish from slaves being flogged around him, shared laughter with their masters, the groans of men cumming.

"So here he is after all," said a familiar voice.

"I told you so," Pete said. "You want him?"

"Sure. For a while anyway."

"Happy birthday, buddy!"

Will was released from the cage. He felt the weight of his leash change hands.

"You're his until I come for you." Pete gave him a brief kiss. "Be good."

Once the blindfold was removed, Will kept his eyes on the floor as he'd been taught. He never looked up at his new master. The party broke up. Will was led outside on his leash. It never occurred to Will to ask his new master's name, or where they were going.

"It was nearly dawn when they left the Catacombs, the sky still a dark blue. Will followed the man down the alley, across a deserted main street, and into another alley. They turned down a side street and into still another alley. Will as hopelessly lost.

He was led up the front steps of a nondescript house on a narrow side street and into its individual darkness. Will's heart beat faster. Despite the fatigue of being kept awake all night, he felt suddenly very alive. It was the way he felt about Folsom, only closer, more intimate than the street. The door closed behind them. Will turned around. In the shadows he saw the face he'd recognize anywhere.

"My name is Aaron. You're a slave, so your name, if you have one, is unimportant. You will not call me by my name, of course. You will only call me 'master' and 'sir.' Do you understand, slave?"

"Yes, sir."

Will was pushed abruptly to his knees. Leather was peeled aside and Aaron's cock shoved down his throat. Grabbing each ear, Aaron rode Will's face with quick, strong strokes. He half drowned Will with his cum, and then again with his piss.

Aaron announced that they were going to bed and ordered Will to follow him up the stairs on all fours. Once upstairs, Will helped Aaron out of his leather, hanging it neatly on a valet. When Will had stripped himself, Aaron secured him to the oak bed frame with leather shackles.

Aaron fell asleep at once, holding Will tightly in his arms. Will felt a half-erect cock rubbing against his body and wondered if he'd be fucked by it. Then he thought of Jay (as he did at some point almost every day), laughed softly and fell asleep.

Will was woken the next morning by the sharp but agreeable discomfort of Aaron's dick pushing into his hole. Before his initiation, being fucked like this without lube or preparation would have felt like rape. Now he adapted to it, controlled the muscles of his sphincter to open for Aaron's cock. There was pain, but it only made his dick hard.

Half awake and half asleep, he felt for those first few moments that he was servitude's perfect vessel, created to accept pain as pleasure, the depository for other men's cum. And Aaron, he half dreamed, was all masters, all cocks, cumming inside of him. He remembered something he'd once heard, of how Eskimo artists believe that the piece of walrus tusk they are carving already contains the figure that will be their work. Their task is only to listen to the tusk whisper its contents to them and remove the extraneous material and find the already perfect carving within. Aaron was the artists in this case, and Will the figure being carved. He had stripped Will down to an essential self by removing the trappings of an assumed persona. He ceased to be Bill, Billy, William or Willy-Boy. He was just 'slave.'

When Pete arrived to take Will home, he found Will naked and lying on his stomach, kissing Aaron's boot and weeping silently because he didn't want to leave. Aaron had hardly laid a hand on Will all weekend except to fuck one hole or the other. It had been his attitude that had captured Will, had made Will his slave. Now, Will would do anything to be Aaron's slave forever. Pete saw this and felt sorry for Will.

"You don't want to keep him?"

"I can't. You know that, Pete."

"Just for a while, then. Until –."

"No. That wouldn't be fair to him. He is pretty, though. Hey, you horny, Pete?"

"Sure."

Pete dropped his pants, laid down on top of Will and fucked him with sharp, piston like motions. He came with a grunt.

"There," said Aaron. "That ought to make him feel better."

Aaron helped Will up as Pete buttoned up his jeans. Moved by the tears in Will's eyes, Aaron kissed them away, held him close and removed the collar.

Will's clothes were returned to him and he dressed himself in silence.

"Thanks again, Pete."

Pete took Will back to his own on place on Hattie Street.

Will had fallen in love with Aaron, and with a slave's instincts knew his love was hopeless.

"Pete, sir?"

"Will?"

"Please, sir."

"Yes?"

"Please whip me, sir."

"With pleasure."

And in the selfish joy of a cat-of-nine-tails, Will forgot the pain in the pit of his stomach, felt it lift as the lashes cut into the skin of his ass and shoulders. When it was over, and Pete had fucked him again, Will slept deeply in Pete's arms. Early the next morning, before Pete awoke, Will wrote a note thanking Pete for the whipping and fucking he had needed so badly. Then he walked home to shower and shave for work.

Will felt that something important had been accomplished. He had served the man who had first sparked in him the need to serve and inspired his true self. A circle had closed and Will felt complete in it. His friends listened when he told them his story. They nodded knowingly, then asked to see the welts to admire them.

"Nice," said Jim.

"The real thing," said Alan.

"Pretty," said Gene.

Will was satisfied for the moment, but knew that his own master awaited, the mythical top man who would one day confine him by power alone. Will was certain it would happen and continued on faith until it did. When it did, and he was at last owned, completed by the enormity of his master's cock inside him, and in constant discomfort to appease his master's whims, he was at peace with himself.

Years later, Will ran into Jay along Church Street. Jay was wearing ill fitting designer jeans and a garishly pink pullover. Will wore only Levis, boots, a leather vest and his slave collar in the warm September afternoon. Jay acted glad to see Will and invited him to sit down for coffee. On discovering that no one else would have him, Jay was desperate to get Will back again. For his part, Will wanted only to look into the unhappy man's face and be reassured of his own happiness.

"It's sick," said Jay pointing at the rings in Will's nipples. "You can't be happy."

Will laughed with honest amusement.

"Why not?"

"Because it's not love to live that way."

"What way, Jay?"

"That way, that *weird* way you live."

Will laughed again.

"You can't feel about him the way you felt about me. Can you?"

"That's for sure. For one thing, I can trust him to tell me the truth. I never could trust you, you're such a liar."

"Well," said Jay without arguing the point. "You may trust him, but do you *love* him like you loved me?"

Will thought a moment while Jay, thinking he had perhaps won Will back, began planning his future lies and infidelities. Will tried to decide if love and trust were the same thing. There was a time when he had loved Jay more than he now loved his master, had loved him with all the passion of first love. But what of it? He trusted his master with his heart where he had never trusted Jay. To say nothing of his joy in being a slave. The thought of returning to Jay was ludicrous, of course, but he enjoyed making the comparison after all this time.

"See? You can't say you love him like you loved me," insisted Jay, interrupting Will's thoughts.

"If trust isn't the same as love, Jay, then it's something akin to love. And I'll take it any day over spending my life with a tired queen like you."

Will stood to go.

"Thanks for the coffee. You'll have to pay for it since I'm not allowed to carry cash without permission."

Once again, Jay was left alone.

JASON, CAT

Perhaps the mouse, between one blow and the next,
has respite enough to appreciate the softness of a cat's paws.

-Colette

<u>You can't tame a cat.</u>

But you couldn't tell Bernie anything either. He thought he knew everything. He always had dogs, too, and in a way that explains why Bernie wanted Jason in the first place: Jason was a cat and couldn't be tamed.

When I first saw Jason he was laying on Bernie's floor, naked. His body was stretched out in the sunlight coming through the window. I remember that his skin was pale, but darkly so, the body lean and neatly muscled, his black hair tousled about like a disobedient child's. He hadn't shaved for a few days and the angles of his face were accentuated by the dark stubble. His chest, stomach, legs, butt and forearms were covered with black hair/fur. His face was handsome with a straight nose and well defined chin. He was nothing less than beautiful.

He appeared to be asleep as I admired him, though I'd never know for certain that he wasn't watching me the whole time from behind his thick black lashes.

Bernie had been my first master, and he always felt a certain responsibility for having brought me out into the scene. He called once a week or so to ask how I was, who I was playing with (and if he disapproved he'd say so) and sometimes suggest that we get together for dinner or a beer. After a while he introduced me to his new slaves and taught me to top by sharing them with me. More than anything else, he was my friend.

When I'd come to see him that morning in his second floor flat, he motioned for me not to talk and nodded towards Jason who lay asleep (we thought) on the floor.

"I'm letting him rest," said Bernie when we'd gone into the kitchen. "I only took the collar off an hour ago. He was so ornery I kept him in chains. He couldn't have gotten much sleep."

"Ornery?" I asked. I couldn't imagine Bernie putting up with any disobedience. I was always slapped silly for any sign of resistance.

"Yeah. It sounds funny, but it feels like he only obeys me when I'm in the room, like he's disobeying even when he isn't. And when I slap him, he glares at me."

"Just like a cat," I said without thinking.

"You and your cats, Jimmy. For a cat-boy you sure loved being a dog.

This was true. I never really liked dogs, though I liked Bernie's shepherd, Max. But being treated like a dog was great. I got off on humiliation, and what could be more humiliating than being called an animal that I didn't even like?

I accepted the coffee Bernie handed me as Jason walked in with more grace than seemed humanly possible.

Bernie is a big man, six-three maybe, barrel-chested, with enormous arms and big hands. He had a beautiful red beard he kept full but neat, was bald on top but furry everywhere else. (One of his other boys and I used to call him Bernie Bear, but never to his face.) He was also a demanding master who knew just how far to push a slave, how to get everything out him. He'd treat you mean, then hold you close and let you feel so safe in his big, brawny arms that you knew the hell he'd put you though had been worth it. At least that's how I always felt with him. The point is, I really loved Bernie, and I doubted this new boy of his appreciated him.

Jason looked at me now and nodded as if he already knew me. He was smaller than Bernie, of course, but taller than me though not as big as me, not as muscular or heavy boned.

"Jason, this is Jimmy. Jim, Jason."

He nodded again in the same way.

"Hi. "

"Coffee?" asked Bernie.

"Feeling okay?" asked Bernie, resting one giant hand on Jason's furry little bottom.

"Yeah," he said as he stretched out his body with the same grace that he'd walked into the room. "Feel great." He gave Bernie a perfunctory kiss.

"Jim and I are going to lunch. Hungry?"

"Sounds good," he said matter-of-factly, as if the invitation were expected. He sat down opposite me and looked directly into my eyes. I looked out the window, already afraid of him. I felt devastated, almost violated, but also elated. And I knew he sensed all this without being told.

The dog, who'd been asleep in the corner of the kitchen until Jason had come in, got up and, almost cowering, backed out his pet door with a low whine to sit with deliberation on the back porch.

"What's his problem?" asked Bernie looking after the dog through the kitchen window.

Jason looked directly into my eyes.

"Dog had a bad dream," he said with calm authority. "Isn't that right, Jim?"

I looked back at him, still awed by his beauty, and grunted agreement.

"What would you know about dogs, Jimmy? Jason, Jim here is cat fancier. Sometimes I think he prefers them people."

Jason's eyes sparked with new interest.

"Really, Jim?"

"Usually," I laughed, trying to make light of it.

"I'm not surprised," said Jason, his voice almost hypnotic. "You're that sort of person." He said the last word with an odd emphasis, as if it were one he was unused to using.

Bernie laughed, apparently thinking that it was all a joke. I laughed with him, but could think only of how I'd do anything for Jason, to feel the strength of our two bodies locked together. How could Bernie want to break him? I'd rather have been Jason's slave, to be played with as cruelly as he pleased, to be his completely. But belonging is a two way street: A master must belong as much as a slave belongs and Jason could belong to no one. I knew all this, but my desire to own him, to be owned by him, was only fueled by its futility as I watched him pad softly out of the kitchen to get dressed.

Jason stayed on my mind. I wondered how I could see him alone, wondered who he really was. When I played with other men, put myself at their mercy, I was never satisfied. I felt nurtured when I wanted, even needed, to feel used. I, who had disliked dogs, became like one, ready to sacrifice myself for my master's affection.

I waited for Bernie to call me, as I knew he would, to confide in me his doubts about Jason. I knew Bernie well enough to know that there would always be doubts.

"I can't figure him, Jimmy."

"He's like a cat, Bernie, and you can't tame a cat."

"You and your cats. If he doesn't to be my slave why is living with me?"

"He is?"

"Didn't I tell you? He's gonna be my slave full time. It's what I want, Jimmy. I love him."

"And him?" I asked, afraid my voice would betray all.

"Who can tell. He's A mystery to me. Sometimes it's as if I'm the one being trained. It's the craziest thing…"

He is a cat, I whispered to myself.

"Where did you meet him, anyway?" I asked aloud, as cool as I could

"At the Catacombs. I'd never seen him there before and he was so pretty I thought he should be treated right on his first visit, so I –"

"Is he from around here?" I interrupted.

"He says from up by the River. But I don't ever remember seeing him up there, do you?"

"No," I answered. "Not that it matters."

Even if I hadn't felt the way I did about Jason, I'd have said that he was bad news for Bernie. But we were both powerless to resist him. Bernie invited me over that evening. I already had a date for later, so I arrived in my leather, feeling pretty hot. My cock was half-erect like it always is when I wear leather next to my skin.

Bernie handed me a beer in the kitchen and we went to the front room where Jason, naked except for his collar and two weeks of a soft, black beard, sat on the floor, his leash tethered to Bernie's big arm chair.

I nodded to Jason as I entered the room. He stared at me with the same open curiosity as before, but revealing nothing. I sat down on the couch, stretched out my legs and looked around the room.

"Where's Max?"

"Out," said Jason with the trace of a smile.

"No one was talking to you, boy," said Bernie without much conviction. "He and Jason don't get along," he said turning to me. "Max is afraid of him."

I watched a brief smile creep over Jason's lips. Sibling rivalry, I thought, and poor Max is loosing.

"Since you're already in your leather and ready for a workout, Jim, why not borrow Jason for a spell. You'd like that?"

I looked at Bernie, then at Jason who was looking up at me instead of at the floor as I would have done in his position, as I was sure Bernie had trained him to do. I knew right away that Bernie's offer was prompted by Jason. He was challenging me. I wavered for only a moment before I remembered what I'd told Bernie: You can't tame a cat.

"Can't tonight, Bernie. Gene's expecting my full attention" I said grabbing my crotch. "I've been saving it for him for a few days so I'll have a lot to give him." I rubbed the leather to show my hard cock. I was ready for some action, but not this action, not the uneasiness I felt in Bernie's house.

Bernie looked relieved and disappointed at the same time. He stroked Jason's hair as if to appease him, not as the kind of condescension I'd expect from Bernie.

"Sure."

"Another night," I lied.

"Sure."

I looked at Jason again. Being naked suited him. Nudity didn't make him look vulnerable at all. He wore his skin the way Bernie and I wore our leather, as an extension of himself. Jason looked back at me with a new expression, not respect exactly, but one that acknowledged me as someone to be dealt with differently than the rest. I let our eyes lock for a moment, holding my stare. For the first time Jason gave himself away. He averted his eyes from mine – as any cat would.

Gene and I were hot that night. Gene was never the kind of guy to play games. He gave all he had, and somehow that was always more than his master expected. He was popular with the crowd I ran with at the Catacombs. He had just the right amount of arrogance that begged to be put in its place, an attitude a lot of tops find hard to resist. Not that he was a pushy bottom, just a good one who expected the best because he was the best. And he always did a top proud.

That night I was crueler than I'd ever been before. With one booted foot, I pushed his face into my other boot. Gene, never presumptuous, waited for permission to kiss the boot. His boot fetish was famous and I denied him the pleasure. Instead I kept my boots just within his reach but forbade him to touch them as I whipped him, watched him squirm and made him beg. But mostly I thought of Jason. This was what Bernie wanted to do to Jason but didn't dare, what I wanted Jason to do to me. When I finally shot my load down Gene's throat for the fifth time, I collapsed on top of him. Together we slept the sleep of the satiated, lost in each other's arms.

Then Max died. Steve mentioned it to me over beers at the Eagle a couple weeks later. The cause of death, he said, was uncertain.

I ran over to see Bernie early the next day. Jason answered the door wearing only a slave collar and cut-off jeans. His beard had grown in and he looked sexier than hell. I made a brief hello and ran back to the kitchen. I found Bernie where I expected to find him, at the kitchen table sitting over a cold cup of coffee.

I sat next to him, took his hand and was silent. We sat together a while before he said anything.

"It's so strange, Jimmy. The animal control people say he was killed by another animal but... He was such a gentle dog..."

I squeezed his hand.

"He broke his neck when he tried jumping over the fence to get away. His collar got caught.,.,"

"I'm sorry, Bernie."

Jason came into the kitchen and poured himself a glass of milk. He moved with the same grace as before. Nothing in his movements or face indicated that he cared about Max or how Bernie might feel. He stopped and looked at me.

"There were claw marks, but to big for a cat. So they think maybe it was rabid raccoon or something. But no one saw anything. Neighbors just heard a lot of noise and called the cops."

"Where were you and Jason, Bernie?"

"I was at the Brig with Jack. Jason was chained up in the basement being punished."

I saw Jason, standing behind Bernie, suppress a smile.

"Did you hear anything, Jason?"

"In the basement? Bernie sound-proofed it. *You* should know that." He did smile this time, and left the kitchen.

"Want some coffee?" asked Bernie.

"No, thanks. I'm okay."

"It's okay, Jim. You don't have to stay. I know you care."

I walked slowly down the steps to the front door, Jason trailing behind me. I held the door open a moment and looked back at him.

"What are you thinking?" he asked.

"I know better than to think, Jason. I already suspect more than I want to."

"That scares you?" he only half asked.

Jason suddenly looked very alert, cocking his head as if he'd heard something. Then I heard it, the sound of Bernie's heavy footsteps above us. Jason looked back to me and gave me a strange smile, a smile that spoke secrets.

"Jason!" Bernie bellowed.

"Yes, sir?"

"Where the hell are you?"

"Down here letting your friend out."

I broke our stare this time, stepping out on to the front porch as Jason closed the door behind me. I heard Bernie's raised voice again, the sound of flesh hitting flesh, and Jason's cry of pain. I walked away fast. I refused to be a witness.

I avoided Bernie and Jason after that, was always "too busy" to talk when he called, unavailable when he wanted to see me. Bernie must have known I was avoiding him, and I'm sure he was hurt. But what could I do? I wanted no part in the drama being played out in that house, so I kept my distance. Bernie, I knew, was unreachable when he was in love. He couldn't hear the truth so there was no point in telling him. I was glad then that he'd only become my big brother instead of my lover.

Gene and I were walking home in the rain from Hamburger Mary's one Sunday morning a few weeks later. We were heading for our respective beds after we'd played most of the night, then gone to breakfast because we knew we were too wired from a sex high to sleep. We were exhausted but happy. I'd gotten more back from Gene than I'd given – and any top will tell how rare that is. I was light headed from the long night and no sleep, but it didn't hinder my mood. I kissed Gene good-by at his front door and turned to go into my place downstairs from him, which is when I saw two two guys (a couple of clones – *not* from our neighborhood) looking over our neighbor's fence calling, "Here, kitty, kitty, kitty!"

I wondered if one of my own cats had gotten out while I was out and asked them what was up. They checked me over a second, me in my leather looking bedraggled and wet on a rainy Sunday morning.

"We thought we saw our cat," one guy said.

"What does it look like?"

"Sorta like a Burmese," the other one said. "But real big."

"Yeah," said the first guy. "We found him up at the River a few months ago and brought him home. He ran away a few weeks later."

"Guess he heard he was getting his balls cut off!" He laughed at his own joke.

"I haven't seen a Burmese around here," I said.

"You know what one looks like?" asked the second guy, apparently skeptical that a leather man should know one kind of cat from another.

Fucking queen, I thought. Go back to your own neighborhood.

"Yes," I said aloud." I have cats of my own. Give me your number and I'll call you if I see it."

One of them handed me a business card

"And the cat's name is Jason."

I shuddered not knowing if it was because I was cold and wet or because of the sound of Jason's name. They thanked me and walked off under their single umbrella as I stood sweating in my leathers. I shook off the uneasiness I felt as I went into my apartment.

Fucking amateurs, I thought. Probably call themselves "cat owners". Dickheads in designer jeans. I'd run away from them, too. Fucking gups.

I stripped off my leathers the moment I got into the door, and tumbled into bed, promising myself I'd give them a proper oiling when I woke up.

I don't know how long it took me to realize that the pounding in my head was really someone pounding at the front door. I looked at my clock; I'd slept an hour. After another five minutes of it I stomped down the hall, still naked, not giving a fuck who was at the door messing with my sleep.

"Yeah?"

It was Jason. He stood naked and wet, disheveled but proud, with only his arms wrapped around himself to keep warm. He nodded a greeting as I pulled him indoors and into the warmth of my flat. I stood him in front of the heater and grabbed a towel from the usual pile of unfolded laundry.

"Here, Jason Let me dry you off."

He was so beautiful I could have licked him dry. He rubbed his body against the towel as I dried his hair. Then I heard it, very distinctly: Jason purred.

I was shivering again.

I pulled a pair or extra blankets from under the pile of laundry and wrapped myself in one as I handed the other to Jason. I pushed the laundry onto the floor and sat on the couch. The purring had stopped. I hoped it had been my imagination, and prayed it hadn't. We were silent a while. I avoided his eyes, half out of respect and half out of fear. Finally he spoke. His voice was deep and quiet, different than it had sounded before.

"Thanks."

"For which?"

"Getting rid of them." He paused and watched my cats enter the room. "They were the last people I expected to meet."

"They were assholes, Jason. I'd leave them, too."

Jason made a deep half-growl towards the cats. They stared at him a moment, then nosed each other as if verifying their shared impressions. Then they sat, albeit cautiously, near the door and watched us through half-closed eyes.

The four of us sat together in the quiet of the rainy afternoon, as cats sit together with each other, demanding and expecting nothing more than each other's company.

Finally I blurted it out, what I'd been afraid to say before,

"I love you, Jason."

I was sure I sounded like A fool.

I expected him to laugh, but he didn't. He only shrugged his shoulders and said, "I know."

We were silent again. A few minutes later, as if it were part of a conversation we'd been having for sometime, he spoke.

"I tried to love Bernie. Only I don't know how. Not the way Max loved him, or the way Bernie loved me. I wanted to belong the way they belong." He motioned to the cats in the corner.

"What are you going to do?"

"Go home. Be with the others."

"Home?" I asked. Others? I thought.

"I only came to say good bye. Because you're my friend. Because you love me."

He came close to me now. My blood ran cold. He was changing. His eyes first, then his face. The soft, silky black body hair increased into fur. He leaned towards me, to kiss me. I leaned away, but he pulled me towards him.

"Jimmy," he growled. "It's what you wanted."

Our mouths met in a kiss. I felt the sharpness of his teeth against my lips, the roughness of his tongue against mine.

Everything went black.

I woke up on the floor, my body spread out in a nest of unfolded laundry. Jason was curled next to me, licking me with his large rough tongue, caressing me with large padded paws. I looked into his face and saw the softness of his beard had grown to cover most of his face. I reached out to stroke the half-human face without thinking. He rubbed his face into my hand, took it into his mouth and chewed it gently as a kitten does when it plays. Then he bit down hard enough to draw blood. I cried out and pulled my hand away.

His face was more human a moment.

"Sorry," he said with a low, guttural purr. Then he licked away the blood.

He purred again and kissed me. I felt his hard cock jab against my thighs with some urgency. I felt his teeth grow sharper and I struggled to get free of the kiss. He held me down and chewed my nipples, his teeth like tiny needles piercing the hardened flesh. He drew blood again, purred with satisfaction and licked it away, like before, with his rough tongue. Then he paused to look at me with cool curiosity and I had the sense that I was prey, to be played with between two gigantic paws.

I wanted to beg him to let me go but couldn't because I also hoped he'd never leave me.

Suddenly I was thrown over on my stomach. He held me down as his nose found my asshole, then his tongue found it, and finally his dick. I screamed louder than I thought possible. I'd been fucked with just spit before, been fucked by cocks bigger than his, and enjoyed it. But I'd forgotten, until I felt his cock pierce my guts, that a cat's dick is barbed.

I felt his body grow furrier as it thrashed on top of mine, felt the disproportionate strength of a cat as he pounded inside of me, tearing me apart. He was getting close I could tell. His sharp, feline teeth bit into the nape of my neck. I screamed again as I felt my flesh tear between his teeth.

Then I wasn't screaming. I succumbed to the blackness surrounding me. I knew Death was fucking me. It was over.

—⁓—

I woke up in my bed the next morning aching all over, my back crusted with blood, tiny scabs covering my tits. I wanted to believe that it had been a dream, but my body was the evidence that said it had been real.

I crawled out of bed and shut the window. The rain had stopped, but a puddle remained on the floor from the night before. Jason, I supposed, had gone out the window and over the roof tops. As I looked out the window, studying the roof tops for a sign of him, I realized that he had put me to bed before he'd left, even tucked me in under the covers. I wanted to believe it was an act of love. All the pain running through my body, pain that would continue for weeks to come, was unimportant now: He loved me.

I called in sick for the entire week, not wanting to explain why I winced each time I stood up, sat down, or took a step. But I savored each pain as it shot through me. Every ache reminded me of Jason, forced another surge of blood into my cock, keeping it erect.

I wallowed in Jason's single act of tenderness. It was my meditation, his name my mantra. And every time I cried out in some sudden reminder of the pain I felt, I loved him more.

When I went to bed that night, and for every night for some time to come, I left the window open, hoping he'd return.

CUTTING THREADS

**The dark furies stalk the man fortunate beyond all right, to
wrench his life aside and drop him into darkness...**

-Aeschylus

Pete had long given up on finding the man who could master him.
Willing bottoms, anxious slaves, were plentiful. A good top he hadn't
met in years. The others, the men who had initiated him, trained him as
a slave and then as a master, had given him his first leathers and taught
him the (then) obscure rituals of a secret world, had for the most part
disappeared. Now he walked the streets, bars and alleys aching for
the lash he gave his own slaves, for the torment he gave others with
such tender affection. Over and over he asked himself, "Where are the
men?"

Pete was not so old (his mid-thirties) that he felt out of date, nor
was he so foolish to believe that things would never change. He was

handsome enough, bearded, well made. He turned a few heads when he went out, he knew, though he often failed to notice. He was attractive to enough men to stay happy without being outstanding.

Tonight he was meeting two boys at the Ambush. He looked forward to the potential dynamics of playing two slaves off of each other, slaves who were already close friends. He would force them to compete against each other, he decided, looking forward to the scene. He arrived early so he could confront them for their tardiness when they arrived on time as he knew they would.

Then Carl appeared.

He wore his leather like the proverbial second skin. Taking off his jacket with the natural grace of an animal, a grace unnatural in a mere man, he revealed his huge arms and chest, each nipple pierced with a gold ring. His knee-high boots were slick with spit and polish, demanding homage. A serpent was tattooed coiling around his left arm, its tail resting on the man's shoulder, its head poised at attention on the biceps. Immaculate in his eroticism, too perfect in Pete's eyes to be real, the stranger stared at Pete as if he'd just given Pete an order and was waiting to be obeyed.

Pete approached him as he would an altar, in reverence and fear, watching the serpent move sensuously over the sleek tanned muscles that moved beneath it. Pete knelt before the man and kissed his boots, wondering to himself if it was the man or the serpent that had just become his god.

A few minutes later, Pete was led down the street on a leash, passing his own boys on their way to meet him. They stared at him, dumbfounded, first in awe and then in contempt. "What had become of our master?" they asked each other as Pete was led past them and down the nearest alley. Pete kept his eyes on the sidewalk, saying nothing.

38

Pete stood in the center of the darkened room, shivering. It seemed an eternity had passed since he'd been left there, his arms in shackles suspended high above his head. Then he heard his master's footsteps somewhere behind him. A voice came out of the shadows:

"Boy."

"Sir."

A gloved hand gently caressed Pete's buttocks.

"I want to take you where you've never been before. But that will take time. And you'll have to trust me."

"Yes, sir."

"You'll have to believe in me, believe that I know what I'm doing, that I'll never hurt you – permanently. Can you do that?"

Pete listened closely, but was distracted by the sensation of feeling aloft. It was not so much the sensation of flight, or even floating, but that he was suspended in space between earth and sky – suspended by the threads that tugged at his nipples, asshole, wrists, ankles, navel and cock, threads that might snap easily, letting him fall into empty space. But even as he looked out into the darkness before him, the darkness behind the blindfold that was now slipped over his face, he knew the answer.

"Yes, master."

He realized that there was no alternative, even if he'd wanted otherwise. He was still the man's mercy and no one knew where he was.

"You're sure?"

The gloved hand continued its gentle stroking, this time up and down Pete's spine.

Pete paused before answering but his answer was more certain than before.

"Yes, sir."

Now he knew, or at least decided that he knew, that he was dreaming.

A riding crop began its slow dance across his ass cheeks, moving softly over the furry mounds, quietly at first, slowly building to a crescendo. The power and pace of the crop's kisses increased methodically.

Pete's arms and legs strained at their restraints as he felt himself writhe in space, suspended. He found himself lost, deep within the maze of his own making. As the crop's tongue bit deeper into his flesh, he remained a viewer to the ritual, detached.

The crop was replaced with a cat-of-nine-tails that sliced still further into his consciousness. He saw the inside of his head as a lattice work, a series of fibers spaced with perfect symmetry allowing for shafts of illumination from within. With each stroke of the whip, the spaces increased, and with them the light, until it seemed that there was no space left to be illuminated. But as he looked into the depths behind the darkness of the blindfold he saw only blackness again, blackness in need of the cat's many tails lashing it into clarity.

He hardly felt the strokes of the whip now. Then not at all.

Time passed and he found himself again touching ground, returning to the world, even as he felt the many threads tugging at him in all directions. He felt his master's arms around him and the man's bearded mouth on his, kissing him deeply, passionately. (And 'passion', he would later remind himself, means 'pain.') He would have to thank the man for the kiss, he thought, but before he could say anything, there were two gloved hands around his throat. All the threads that held him went slack. He fell into empty space.

His lips no longer felt his master's lips, though Pete knew that his master was still there, still kissing him as he fell into the void. He fell faster into the yawning darkness.

No, he remembered, I need to thank my master for the kiss.

He was immersed in a tangible blackness.

I must remember...

Pete woke up in the stranger's massive arms. By the light he saw through the crack of a window, Pete guessed it to be early afternoon.

Pete's entire body ached. He tried to stretch and discovered that his wrists and ankles were still bound. It was then that he also realized that he was being fucked, ever so sweetly, with long rocking strokes. "I love you already, sweet man," Carl whispered, fucking Pete harder than before. "I'll give it to you right."

At first, Carl didn't want Pete to leave.

"If you go it is without my consent."

"Please, sir. I have responsibilities, a job, friends..."

"Those were forsaken when you chose to be my slave."

"That wasn't made clear, sir."

"It was implicit. You knew."

Pete gave up trying to reason.

"Sir, come on –"

A back hand sent Pete across the floor. Dazed, he pulled himself up. Blood trickled across his lips. He could only stare at the man who stood between him and the door.

"Crawl on your belly and kiss the underside of my boot and beg my forgiveness."

Pete obeyed.

"Please forgive me, sir. It won't happen again, sir. I know I'm a worthless slave, sir."

"No, not worthless," said Carl. "Only disobedient."

Carl lifted Pete to his feet.

"All right, Pete. You can go. But you will be back here on Friday evening at exactly seven o'clock. You will continue to wear my collar in the mean time. If you take it off, you'll wish you hadn't. You will also decide in that time whether or not you wish to continue being my slave. If you choose to go on, as I expect you will, you won't return to the outside world again except as I see fit. Do you understand me, Pete?"

"Yes, master."

"Questions?"

"No, master."

"Now put your clothes on and get out of here before I change my mind."

"Yes, sir."

Carl left the room.

Once Pete stepped back into the fading sunlight of the street, he spent several aimless minutes wandering the alleys before he got his bearings again. In the two days he'd spent with Carl, he'd forgotten about so much: how to live, where he lived, his job, his friends.

Each step of the walk home reminded him of how severely he'd been beaten. While he winced in pain, he was content with it, as if it were a precious gift. Being in pain let him feel closer to his master.

The night before he'd been taken out on a leash, used as a footstool in one bar while Carl smoked a cigar, then tethered to a hydrant and left outside like a dog at another. At no point had he protested or attempted to escape. It had all seemed, like his pain, perfectly natural.

Friends called him for several days, some desperate to know what had become of him, others angry over broken dates. Pete was evasive with everyone, telling no tales of where he'd been, even to his closest friends. He remained aloof, refused to see anyone, telling himself that he didn't want to explain to anyone the stiffness in his body or the bruises around his throat. The truth, though, was that Carl had displaced Pete's entire life even if Pete was not yet ready to admit it.

"You're a master in your own right, aren't you, Pete?"

Pete hesitated before deciding on the truth: "Yes, master."

A gloved hand softly touched Pete's bowed head. Pete leaned his face against his master's thigh.

"You'd have to be a master, Pete, or they'd be no point in training you."

"Sir?"

"You don't understand me, do you?"

"No, master."

"You will in time."

"Thank you, sir."

"You'd like to know more, wouldn't you?"

"Yes, sir."

"I want you to serve me, Pete –"

"Yes, sir!"

Pete felt a strong tug on his collar, almost choking him.

"Don't interrupt me, slave!"

"Yes, master. I'm sorry, master." His voice broke.

"As I was saying, boy, I want you to serve me in a very specific way. I will require it only once of you, and when it's done you will be freed forever. But you need to be prepared for it, Pete, or you won't make it. You need to understand, to become a different person, more like me. In a way, you'll become me."

He spoke without bravado or pretense, but there was a deliberate casualness in his tone that demanded attention.

"Yes, master. I'll always obey you, sir."

And Pete was content at that moment, kneeling at his master's feet, smelling the leather of his master's presence. He was also content with himself. Good slaves like me are rare, he thought, not the pushy kind.

"But, master, you said I could stay. Please let me stay, sir."

Pete laid his cheek on Carl's boot. Carl, who was sitting back with his long muscular legs stretched out in front of him, suddenly pulled his boot from under Pete and rested it instead on the back of his slave's neck.

"What I said, slave, was that you wouldn't leave again unless I wished it. I am leaving your collar on you, so there is no need to worry. But if you argue with me, I'll remove the collar and toss you out on your worthless ass. Is that clear, boy?"

"Yes, master."

"Because you've angered me, you will be punished."

"Yes, master. Thank you, sir."

But Pete was devastated by the punishment. No riding crop sliced the air into his buttocks. No whip danced along his spine. He was sent out into the cool of the night without so much as a touch, without the life giving kiss he constantly craved from Carl but received only so often, between assaults, to keep him hungry.

Pete turned back to plead with Carl for one tender touch.

"Get out!"

Pete heard his master's steps fade away behind the locked door. He walked home in complete despair.

When Pete returned the following weekend, Carl acted as if nothing had happened. Pete found comfort in this benign neglect, proof of his master's compassion.

As weeks passed, Pete was whipped with increasing brutality, but he felt only more content, less anxious, as the pain increased. Like a trained athlete, he adjusted to the pain, or at least enough to be unaware of it. He took pride in the bruises that covered his body and ringed his neck. Each fuck climaxed with Pete choking for air, then coming to consciousness in Carl's arms. Each time he woke to Carl's soothing deep voice saying, "It's all right, baby. Daddy brought you back." Then Carl would kiss him and Pete felt restored, felt the kiss fill him again with what had been drained from him.

It went on for months. Each time he served his master, Pete found himself suspended in space again, suspended by invisible threads. The threads, he came to realize, never broke but were only released like the strings of a marionette. Each time he fell into the blackness, plunged into the nameless ocean somewhere deep inside himself, he re-emerged in Carl's arms again, panting like an exhausted swimmer.

"You've gone where no one else has taken you."

"Yes, sir."

"And I bring you back each time, don't I?"

"Yes, master."

"You trust me to know that I always will?"

Pete dared to look up into his master's face without permission. Tears threatened the corners of his eyes.

"Yes, master!"

"Kiss your master's hand."

Pete was taken out on the leash with increasing frequency, and to places other than Folsom Street. First they walked to Polk Street, crossing Market Street at rush hour. Then they went to the Castro on a Sunday afternoon. On a holiday weekend Pete was sent to a supermarket on Chestnut Street in a tank shirt and slave collar. Pete knew that people from his office would, and did, see him on these expeditions, but he cared less and less about what others thought.

On an evening, dressed in coat and tie, Carl put Pete in handcuffs, attaching a leash to them, for a stroll down Union Street. The only thought in Pete's mind as he heard the murmur of shock and recognition from passerby, was that he be allowed to lick his master's shoes in a well lit place for everyone to see.

Seasons changed. The rains came. Friends who had given up hope of getting in touch with Pete during the summer tried again, assuming that there'd been a romance that would naturally end come autumn. Pete only said that he had "no free time," that he was "too busy" to see them. Inevitably they were offended. Soon no one called Pete but Carl. Now Pete, to his joy, could answer the phone "Yes, sir!" every time.

They were sitting together, as they often did, Carl in his chair, Pete on the floor nestled between his master's legs. It was a Sunday afternoon and Pete didn't want to go home yet. He hoped his master would allow him to stay an extra night, as sometimes happened, but he didn't dare to ask.

"You will not see me for a month, slave."

"Master?" Pete' stomach suddenly tied itself into knots. Tears came to his eyes. He hoped Carl was only playing a cruel joke on him.

"A month."

"Sir, have I –."

"No, slave, you haven't displeased me in anyway."

Pete said nothing now. He waited in silence, resting his cheek on Carl's leather clad leg. Minutes passed.

"You see, slave, I have a special task for you."

Pete's eyes brightened in hope. "Yes, sir!"

"You are to be a master again."

"Sir?"

"I'm giving you your freedom for a month. In exactly four weeks it will have been a year since I put my collar on you."

Pete nuzzled Carl's legs like an affectionate pet.

"Yes, sir."

"When you come back to me on that day, I'll ask one last thing of you. You may choose not to carry it out, but I anticipate that you will. I've prepared you so carefully."

Pete was puzzled at words like 'ask' and 'choose.' It was as if he might disobey his master, something he could never imagine.

Carl stroked Pete's head.

"When you've completed what I'll ask of you, you will become... something more than you are now. But you don't understand me, do you, boy? Don't worry, you will."

"Yes, master."

They sat together in contented silence as the room darkened and daylight failed. Finally, half an hour later, Carl broke the silence.

"I want you to know something, Pete. I love you very much."

These were the words Pete hung on, always hoped for, but never expected, each time they came. Blind with gratitude, he licked Carl's gloved hand like a dog receiving praise.

Carl took a key from his vest pocket. As he held Pete's face close to his in a long, quiet, kiss, he unlocked the collar and very gently laid it aside.

"All right, Peter. It's time for you to go."

The next evening, Pete's phone rang. He jumped out of his chair, startled by the noise. He looked blankly at the phone a moment. He knew it wasn't Carl. Who would be calling him now after all these months?

"Hello?"

"Pete! It's Jack."

Pete knew at once, remembered playing with his asshole, how well he took a beating, and that he was a good fuck. Jack, he also remembered, was handsome and appreciative of a master's efforts, being a top himself. He hadn't seen Jack in over a year.

"So how's that sweet butt of yours, Jacky-Boy?"

"Needs a licking bad, daddy. I was hoping maybe you could take me in hand again. I know it's been a while, sir, but I tried calling you a lot and you were never home–."

"Been busy," Pete interrupted. What about Friday?"

"Hey, all right!"

"What was that, fuckhead?"

"Yes, *sir!*"

"That's better."

"Yes, sir."

"And, boy?"

"Yes, sir?"

"Better keep the whole weekend free."

"Yes, sir! Thank you, sir!

As Pete hung up the phone he caught his reflection in the mirror and saw in it what had been missing for so long: The glint in his eye that said "master."

He stripped off his office clothes and looked at his body naked a moment. The bruises and welts were healing rapidly now, some that he was sure were weeks old but never allowed to heal before. Certain that Carl had been no easier on him than before over their last weekend together, he wondered at the sudden change. But Pete had learned to accept many things he didn't understand over the last eleven months. This new oddity, the sudden healing of old wounds, was just one more to take in stride.

He put on his leathers again, something he'd been forbidden since Carl had enslaved him. They fit better than he remembered. He felt the power of the leather as his cock hardened. Still looking at his reflection in the mirror, he stroked his cock while playing with his nipples. He shot like a geyser, covering the glass with cum.

Pete met Jack at the Ambush. He'd been away nearly a year and had been missed. Old friends wanted to know where he'd been hiding. Pete continued to be evasive.

When Jack arrived on time, Pete was already there waiting and slapped Jack hard across the face as punishment for being late, though they both knew it was a pretense. A moment later Jack was groveling on the floor licking Pete's boots. In another moment Pete was leading Jack up Harrison Street on a leash, all to the murmured admiration of the crowd.

Pete was never so attentive as he was that night with Jack. Even as he felt a certain detachment to the muffled cries coming from Jack's gagged throat, Pete watched Jack's face and body, reading them for signals, anticipating Jack's needs to the second. He saw Jack in his mind's eye as well as before him, saw him suspended in space by myriad threads held taught by the pain in his body, by the whip in Pete's hand.

When Pete saw the look of peace come over Jack's face, saw that he was euphoric and on the other side of pain, he gently removed the gag. Holding Jack's face between his two hands, as Carl has so often held his, Pete kissed Jack and felt him return to Earth through his kiss. That was the moment.

"Don't worry, baby. Daddy's here."

Pete's hands closed around Jack's throat as they kissed. Pete saw Jack falling into nothingness, into the blackness, as he had fallen so often with Carl. Then Pete let go, breathed life back into Jack with his kiss, brought him back to the surface from the beneath the waves of a primal sea.

"You're back, baby. Daddy brought you back."

"Sir," was the hoarse reply.

Pete kissed him again.

"Thank you, sir," Jack sighed, his voice clearer now. "Thank you..."

Now Pete was ready to fuck him.

Carl never called. The fourth Sunday arrived and there had been no word at all. Pete hadn't expected Carl to call, but he hoped for it each time the phone rang. Even with his rediscovery of his status as a master, he felt a part of himself missing, the part held aloft by invisible threads at the end of Carl's whip.

When he walked to Carl's house on Sunday afternoon, he almost got lost, forgetting the exact side street. He wore his leather, enjoying the feel of it, as well as the sound of his own boots clicking against the dirty pavement. He accidentally walked past the house, then back tracked to it to find the door ajar.

The house was in perfect order, like a house cleaned for inspection by a new owner. Pete turned on the light, called for Carl and, getting no answer, followed his intuition to the high ceilinged room that had been the center of his life with Carl.

Hanging on the doorknob he found a slave collar, unlocked. He held it in his hand and opened the door. He found Carl kneeling on the floor under a single light, naked, his head bowed, his hands behind his back.

"Carl?"

"Sir?"

"Look at me, Carl."

Carl obeyed.

Not quite understanding but following his instincts, Pete pulled his former master up by his hair and secured the collar around his neck. Tight.

"Does that feel better, boy?"

"It feels right, sir."

Pete gave Carl the back of his hand and sent the man sprawling on the floor.

"Is this what you wanted all along? Why didn't you just tell me, fuckhead?"

"I had to show you first, sir. I had to show you where I needed to go..."

Carl's eyes pleaded more than his words. Pete was strangely touched by the intense longing within them. He spoke gently now.

"You want to fall from where you were, slave?"

"Yes, sir."

"To feel suspended in space and then fall into you own soul, through the darkness until you see the light?"

"Yes, master. *Please!*"

Carl's eyes pleaded like a dumb animals for food.

"You're ready to let me hold the threads? You'll trust me to bring you back?"

Carl kept his eyes on Pete's boots, but said nothing.

"I asked you a question, slave."

"Please, sir. Don't hold on, sir."

Pete wasn't sure that he wanted to understand.

"Don't bring me back, sir. Let me fall, sir. Forever, sir. *Please, master!*"

Carl groveled at Pete's feet. Pete understood now, completely. Pete looked straight ahead into the darkness of the room and spoke calmly to the sniveling wreck on the floor.

"Cut the threads and let you fall."

"Yes, sir. Please, sir."

"Snip, snip."

"Please, master."

"And all this, this house?"

"Yours, sir."

"Whose was it before?"

"My master's, sir."

"And before him?"

"His master's, sir."

Pete understood again. Completely. While he wondered where and how this had all begun, and whether (or even, if) it would ever end, he already knew that there was no escape. He had been, if not caught in the web, then drawn to it by instinct, by what he knew he himself needed. This was it.

He looked down now at the man trembling on the floor, eager and afraid, with anticipation.

"Yes."

"Thank you, master."

There was no escape now, except to follow Carl and the others, to fall free of the web into the darkness, to cut the threads that had held him all his life. He envied Carl now, envied him his journey.

Pete pushed one booted foot into the slave's face.

"Kiss it," said Pete. "Kiss your master's boot."

TYKE

***What is the point of being a little boy if you are
growing up to be a man.***

- Gertrude Stein

Tyke was curled up on the carpet at Daddy's feet. If his wrists hadn't been cuffed behind his back, Tyke might have reached out to caress Daddy's boots with his hands, then perhaps with his cheek, and finally with his lips and tongue. This was a kindness usually allowed him, but Tyke had been bad that day. Tyke had been late for work that morning. Again.

"Why were you late, boy?"

"I overslept, sir. You kept me up so late I –."

"Don't talk back to me, boy!"

"Yes, sir."

Tyke had been punished: stripped of his clothes, taken to the shed and whipped. Worst of all, Daddy had threatened to find another boy to fuck instead of Tyke.

"I'll tie you up and make you watch, boy. Maybe that will teach you."

"Please don't, Daddy. I'll be good."

"We'll see."

Once Daddy had gone out looking for another boy, but to Tyke's relief the man came home alone. Tyke had been so happy on that occasion that he didn't mind being hog-tied and left on the floor for the night with only a scratchy wool army blanket for warmth.

Daddy put down his paper and looked at Tyke. His face was expressionless. Tyke felt his throat dry up. He licked his lips and kept his eyes on the floor. A booted foot gently nudged Tyke over onto his stomach. Tyke knew better than to tense his body in anticipation, even as he heard the wooden paddle slice the air before landing hard across his ass cheeks. He stifled a sob.

Daddy got out of his chair.

Tyke heard the sound of Daddy's leather jacket creak as he put it on, then Daddy's footsteps heading down the front hall. The door opened and closed. A moment later Tyke heard the sound of Daddy's truck start up and drive down the hill.

Tyke's heart was in his throat.

He sat up as best he could in his restraints. With some effort he managed to get on his feet and stumble to the window. He could just make out the lights of their nearest neighbors through the trees.

The lock on his collar felt heavy on his neck, which is only to say that he was aware of it for the first time in months. He'd worn it for over two years and rarely thought of it now. Even in the summer months when the area was full of vacationers from the City and the weather so hot that Tyke wore the heavy chain around his neck with only cut-off jeans and sneakers.

Tyke liked to remember how it happened, how he'd met Daddy and left the city streets to live with him here in the country. Since he'd found his Daddy – or rather, been found by him – Tyke's short life had become his own favorite story.

He used to be called Tim, or Timmy if you knew him well, until Daddy called him Tyke. From the first time Daddy had said it, it had been his name. It was so simple. It fit him like his own skin, and as effortlessly as the slave collar.

He'd not been a hustler exactly, though he did depend on the kindness of others. For a meal he was willing to bend over in an alley way long enough to get fucked. If he liked a man, like the way he smiled or said his name, he'd lay on his back somewhere and kiss the man as well, or maybe offer him the use of his mouth and throat.

Being a boy getting by as best he could on the streets, another runaway coming of age in the worst of conditions, unskilled and taking odd jobs and smiles from strangers, he accepted the offer without qualm.

"Come to my party next week. A bunch of guys will be there. I'll give you fifty bucks and all you have to do is lay there."

Tyke tried to refuse the money. It seemed dishonest to accept it when he knew he'd do just as much for no more than the chance to be touched.

The man insisted, though. "You'll earn it."

Tyke was too naive to understand. Even when he arrived at the man's flat off of Harrison Street and was led down a narrow flight of stairs to a room with no windows, he didn't understand.

The room was filled with dangling chains, some suspending a sling. The walls were covered with whips and hardware so strange Tyke couldn't begin to guess their intended uses. In the center of the room was an incline with an ancient, smelly mattress strapped to it.

Tyke stripped and laid down as he was told, stretching out his arms and legs so that they could be secured to leather cuffs at each corner of the incline. It was only then, after he was secured, that he became afraid.

"Looks good," said his host giving Tyke's ass a slap just to see the boy flinch.

Tyke looked around the room and suddenly understood. He'd heard some of the boys on Polk Street talk about this, but he had never believed their stories. He struggled against the restraints, cried, begged to be released.

"Keep it up, kid. The guys'll love it."

A dirty sock was shoved in Tyke's mouth and, with another slap on the ass, the man went upstairs to open the door for his guests.

Tyke heard the heavy scraping of booted feet on the floor above him. In time he heard the sound grow nearer as they thumped down the stairs to the windowless room where Tyke laid prone and helpless. There were hoots of appreciation for the small white buttocks. Rough hands pulled the cheeks apart, slapped them and laughed when Tyke squirmed or fought against his shackles. The men thought his resistance was part of the show, like the faked orgasms of a high priced whore.

The host asked who'd like to go first and "break in the pretty little hole."

Tyke heard the men cheer as one stepped forward to do the honors, then the sound of jangling belts and of leather being peeled from flesh. Tyke held his breath.

Tyke was fucked without ceremony or tenderness, each man more brutal than the one before him, each man needing to hear Tyke's muffled cries to his own satisfaction.

After a time, Tyke felt none of it, but instead floated above the scene, detached, and watched the host bring out a bullwhip to crack over Tyke's ass. Tyke was jarred back into the world by the sound of his own scream. The men laughed to see him writhe against the filthy mattress, blind to the reality of his tears.

"Hey," said the host. "Who wants another beer?"

There was a noisy approval and the pack marched back up the narrow stairs. Tyke returned to the ceiling of the windowless room, watching over his own trembling body.

Tyke was woken up hours later by the sound of his own sobbing under the smack of a belt against his bare ass. He sensed (or perhaps remembered) that he was alone with a single man, and remembering, was more afraid than before. This man intended to hurt him, he knew, and not as the others had in the communal pleasure of what they had supposed to be some internal drama being acted out for Tyke's (or perhaps their host's) benefit. This man wanted to hurt Tyke because he could, because Tyke was alone and unprotected.

Suddenly, a voice filled the room:

"Leave the kid alone!"

"Find your own meat, shithead!"

Tyke heard a scuffle, heard the full weight of a man hit hard against the concrete floor. Terrified of the struggle's outcome, he prayed to an unknown god for deliverance.

"It's okay, boy. Daddy will get you out of here."

Tyke was released, and for the first time saw his savior. He was a large boned man, blonde, clean shaven and handsome. Though not very tall, he was muscular and broad shouldered, giving an impression of height. His lips were thin and tight, his eyes an icy blue.

The man smiled at Tyke and ran a large hand through the boy's long brown hair. Tyke dared to smile at the man through his tears, his brown eyes shining hope. The man wiped away the tears as he looked into the puppy-dog eyes begging for love.

"Poor tyke."

Tyke was allowed to leave the party only after some argument. The host insisted that he be paid back his one hundred dollars, even if Tyke had only been promised fifty dollars he'd never seen. Cash changed hands, however, and Tyke was led out of the house to the shabby street below. Daddy opened the door of his pickup truck, paused a second, then motioned Tyke to join him. Tyke scrambled into the seat and, as it somehow seemed appropriate, licked Daddy's hand in gratitude. The man chuckled softly as he gently pulled his hand away and put the truck in gear.

Tyke sat silently, looking out the window at the passing scenery. They drove north, over the Golden Gate Bridge and beyond, for over an hour. After a while, the truck left the main highway and sped into the hills, past small towns and through acres of forests. Eventually they came to a house lost in the surrounding trees. This was home.

That night a dog collar of heavy chain was fastened around Tyke's neck, secured with a lock that, Daddy assured him, had no key. In the passing years Tyke's body hardened into a lean, supple musculature. His face lost its boyish softness as the features of a young man emerged. The eyes, though, remained the same: big, soft, brown, and pleading.

Tyke was frightened. Daddy was out looking for another boy, he was certain. He laid down and tried to sleep. Curled up on the carpet again in front of the fireplace, he hoped to doze off and wake up in his Daddy's arms, all forgiven.

As his mind wandered, as the logs in the fireplace fell in the grating, he heard every sound from the two lane highway at the foot of the hill. His heart raced when he heard two trucks, his Daddy's and a second, pull up in front of the house. Tyke could hear two men talking. He hoped it was one of Daddy's friends with Daddy, one of the men who periodically borrowed Tyke as a favor from Daddy.

Daddy came into the house with a man Tyke had never seen before, a burly, red bearded man. They came into the house together, arms around each other like old buddies. On seeing Tyke, the man stopped and looked the boy over.

"That him?"

"I'm afraid so, Bernie, though I hate to admit it."

Bernie got down on one knee to pet Tyke as he might pet a dog.

"This boy bad? No..." He ruffled Tyke's hair. "I can't believe it."

"I'm glad you think so." Daddy suddenly changed his tone.

"Boy! Where are your manners? Say 'hello' to your Uncle Bernie."

"Hello, sir."

Tyke liked Uncle Bernie already and hoped that Daddy would let the man fuck him soon. Tyke didn't always like Daddy's friends, or the way Daddy brought him to card games and passed him around among the men so they use him and laugh at him.

Bernie continued petting the boy.

"Such a fine boy."

"Up on your knees!" barked Daddy.

"Yes, sir."

As he got to his knees, Tyke opened his mouth and faced Uncle Bernie who was now undoing his pants and taking out his dick.

"Kiss it first," said Uncle Bernie. "Let it know you care."

Uncle Bernie took Tyke away with him that night. He was taken away in the back of a pick-up truck, still bound and naked. The only difference was the addition of a gag.

He stayed with Uncle Bernie for two weeks. Days were spent in shackles secured by long chains to the wall of the basement. When

Bernie came down to Tyke in afternoon, Tyke would be kneeling in an appropriately submissive pose. Bernie would smile kindly at Tyke, ask him how he had spent his day, slap him if he complained of boredom, then fuck his face.

After eating his dinner out a dish on the floor while Bernie ate his at the kitchen table reading his newspaper, Tyke cleaned the kitchen and rejoined Bernie in the living room. The rest of the evening was spent either as a pet curled up on the carpet or as a footstool supporting Uncle Bernie's booted feet. This last task Tyke took so seriously, and with such pleasure, that his cock remained hard the entire time.

Sometimes Tyke was whipped or tortured. This was never a punishment, however. Tyke was only tormented for the pleasure it gave Bernie. When Bernie was satisfied, and Tyke quivering and tear faced, Bernie would fuck Tyke as he cooed soft words of comfort.

Each night was spent in Bernie's arms. Tyke felt safer in this man's arms than he had ever felt with his Daddy.

"Get up and answer the door, boy," said Uncle Bernie when the doorbell rang on the last afternoon. "That'll be your Daddy."

Tyke, his face and entire body shaved clean just that morning, obeyed immediately.

"Hello, sir," he said, kneeling at once to kiss Daddy's boots.

"I like what you've done with him," said Daddy. "He should always be kept shaved."

"I thought you'd like it," said Bernie.

Daddy pulled Tyke up by his hair, kissed him softly, then slapped him hard across the face.

"Hello, boy."

Tyke waited, bound and blindfolded once again, listening quietly as Daddy and Uncle Bernie spoke together in low tones he could never quite make out. Somehow, he got the impression that money was changing hands, but from whom to whom he neither knew nor understood.

After a while Tyke was led outside into the cab of Daddy's truck. He obediently curled up on the floor as he was told.

"No," he heard Uncle Bernie say. "You won't have any trouble with him now."

"Then I have you to thank."

Daddy got into the truck and they drove off.

At first Tyke assumed that they were heading home. He couldn't tell where they were headed, of course, but after a while something began to feel very wrong. Daddy muttered what sounded like directions beneath his breath. The truck kept turning in and out of poorly paved streets with a seeming randomness that gave Tyke the impression of wandering through a maze.

Then the truck stopped. Tyke was pulled up onto the seat beside Daddy.

"Whatever happens, boy, do as your told and don't say a word. You'll make your Daddy proud."

Tyke only nodded.

Daddy honked the truck's horn a few times before removing Tyke's blindfold. Tyke saw that they were parked in a blind alley. Suddenly, a large van appeared behind them. Daddy swore quietly.

Tyke looked at Daddy and saw for the first time how nervous he was, that his brow and upper lip were dotted with sweat. Tyke was even more puzzled than before.

"Remember, boy. Just do what your told."

"Yes, sir."

"And no lip."

Tyke nodded.

Daddy got out of the truck and stood by the door, waiting for something. Tyke wanted to turn around and look but didn't dare. Instead, he watched through the rear view mirror.

He saw two men get out of the van, their faces covered by black ski masks. One of the men approached the truck on Tyke's side. Tyke held his breath and kept his eyes down. Tyke knew better than to meet the eyes of such men until told.

"This him?"

"Yeah."

"Get out," ordered the man quietly.

Tyke looked to Daddy who, still looking uncomfortable, nodded his concurrence. Tyke obeyed, stood before the man with the perfect posture Daddy demanded. His eyes stayed focused into empty space somewhere beyond his feet. An appraising hand caressed Tyke's firm, neatly muscled body. He was ordered to spread his legs, to bend over, to spread his ass cheeks for the stranger's inspection. Tyke obeyed without thought. When ordered, he stood up again, obeying naturally and without hesitation.

"Look at me."

Tyke obeyed and met a pair of searching green eyes. Without warning, Tyke was slapped hard across the face. Tyke held his gaze as ordered.

"Very good," said the man. "Very well trained."

"I do my best," said Daddy.

"Yes," said the man. "I think we can work something out. But what's the problem with him?"

"No problem," said Daddy. "He's just getting older than I'd like is all."

Tyke began to understand.

The man said nothing, only nodded to the other masked man.

Suddenly Tyke felt a leather hood being pulled over his face. Before he could call out, a gag was inserted through the hood's mouth opening and secured with a strap. Just as suddenly, he felt himself being lifted in a pair of strong arms and carried away. Tyke wanted to call out even if no one would hear him, to promise Daddy anything if only he'd take Tyke home again. But Tyke stayed silent because he wanted to make his Daddy proud.

Tyke felt himself being lowered onto a padded surface. His ankles were secured, than bound to his wrists. A gentle hand caressed him as if to reassure him.

"Don't worry," a new, kinder voice said. "We'll find you another Daddy, one who will love you."

Van doors were slammed shut around him. Then he heard the first stranger's voice again.

"Keep the motor running. I'll show him the catalogue and make the deal. Then we'll send you back for the exchange."

"Yes, sir," said the second voice, the one that had been so kind a moment before. "I'll see that the poor tyke gets special treatment."

Tyke lay where he was, not moving, or even thinking about his predicament. He thought instead of the promise that had just been made to him: Someone would love him.

OFFICER BELTMAN

**When I saw Eros on his way down from heaven,
he wore a soldier's cloak dyed purple.**

-Sappho

Jim never felt really safe walking to the Catacombs at night, and always wished he'd taken a cab from Folsom Street when he did. It wasn't until he was within a block of Shotwell Street that he'd feel confident again. Except this time, when he spotted a cop car tucked neatly into an alley, it's lights off. Thinking this odd, he approached the car slowly, and saw that there was also a motorcycle. He hesitated only for a moment before peering around the corner.

The motorcycle cop was leaning against the wall, his helmet, gloves and jacket all in place. The other policeman, the one from the patrol car, was on his hands and knees licking the other's knee high boots.

"Come on," said the motorcycle cop undoing his pants and pulling out a thick uncut cock. "We don't have much time."

The second cop opened his mouth and swallowed it whole as the motorcycle cop planted both gloved hands behind his head and fucked. Jim heard the cocksucker choke, but the motorcycle cop either didn't notice or didn't care. He grunted as he held the patrolman's head close and pumped a load down his thirsty throat. Pulling the cock out of his fellow cop's mouth and stuffing it back into his uniform, he put one booted foot on the other's shoulder and sent him sprawling on the filthy pavement.

"Get up, cocksucker. You're getting your uniform dirty."

"Yes, sir."

Both policeman saw Jim at the same time.

"Sir?" said the patrolmen to his partner.

"Get out of here. I'll take care of him."

"Sir, I –."

"I said, get out of here!"

"Yes, sir."

Jim could see them better now. The cocksucker looked like your basic clone, only in uniform – average build, probably well muscled beneath the uniform, but to Jim's mind less a man than the one who'd just mastered him. The top man was handsome, square-jawed and built as solid as a house. A thick brown mustache threatened to cover his lips, which were thick and sensual.

"Come here, boy."

"Sir."

The patrol car pulled out of the alley and took off.

"You see it all, boy?"

"Most of it, sir."

The policeman stroked Jim's face with a gloved finger.

"You're a good looking boy."

Jim said nothing at the compliment, waiting for a cue from the cop as to how he should behave. Suddenly, a gloved hand smacked Jim hard across the face.

"Don't you know how to say 'thank you,' boy?"

"Yes, sir. Thank you, sir."

"That's better."

He pulled out his notebook and took down Jim's name, address and phone number.

"You know how to suck cock, boy?"

"Yes, sir."

"Good. You'll be hearing from me soon."

"Thank you, sir."

Jim told his friends what had happened as soon as he got to the Catacombs, and though many had heard similar stories before, or read them in magazines, no one believed him. Nearly everyone had tricked with a cop, of course, been his slave or his master, but no one, outside of a dirty movie, had actually seen two cops fucking in an alleyway. One man even claimed to know the whole police force intimately and insisted that there was no one on the force fitting Jim's description.

"How would you know, queen?" spat Jim. "When was the last time you got off your knees long enough to see a guy's face?"

After that Jim kept the story to himself, except when he was talking to Gene, who accepted Jim's story with quiet enthusiasm. He asked for details not to verify the factualness of the story, but to understand all its erotic possibilities

The next Sunday afternoon, Jim was lying on the floor of his flat listening to music and wondering if he should bother getting dressed and go to the Eagle. He was about to get up and call Gene to see if he was going when he heard the roar of two motorcycles stopping in the street outside his window. The motor's died and the unmistakable sound of a police radio was heard. He was just going to look out the window when there was a loud knock on the door. He froze, half eager and half afraid. The knock came again, louder this time.

He answered the door, catching his breath when he saw who it was: The motorcycle cop from the alley with a second officer, a man as big and sturdy as himself.

"James Cash?" asked the policeman, very business like.

Jim nodded yes and wondered what was up.

"I'm Officer Beltman, this is Officer Jackson. We have some business with you." The two men pushed their way inside. Jackson locked the door behind them as Beltman grabbed Jim and dragged him down the hall where he was handcuffed and forced to his knees.

"First of all, fucker," said Officer Beltman. "When a police officer asks you a question, you answer it with the word 'sir.' Is that understood, boy?"

"Yes, sir."

"I still think he needs to be punished," said Jackson.

"Sure he does, but after I get my rocks off."

Officer Beltman undid his fly and pulled out the same fat hose Jim had seen that night in the alley. It seemed so much bigger up close, almost frightening.

"He says he can suck cock. We'll see. Open up, faggot."

Jim obeyed and the full length of Beltman's cock was shoved into place, filling Jim's mouth and throat. Jim tried to breathe between thrusts, but it only got more difficult as the cock got harder and fatter with the brutal pounding his mouth got. Eventually, the mammoth head expanded in Jim's throat and prevented him from breathing at all. Jim felt himself black out as ribbons of cum exploded down his gullet. He tried to breathe but choked on the cum instead, inhaling it into his windpipe. When Beltman pulled out his dick as roughly as he'd shoved it in, Jim was in a fit of coughing.

"What's his problem?" asked Officer Jackson.

"Don't ask me. Guess he's kind of a sissy. That right, boy?"

"Yes, sir," Jim answered between coughs, still gasping for air.

"What's that, boy?"

"Yes, sir!"

"Better."

"Hey, man," said Jackson. "I need to get my nut off, too. Gonna share it with me?"

"Help yourself."

Jackson pulled Jim up by his hair and bent him over a chair. Jim's Levis were torn off of him. Jim heard the officer spit and rub it on his cock. Then there came the burning and tearing of Jackson's monster dick ramming into his unlubed hole. Jim screamed with pain, trying to escape the assault, but Officer Beltman held him down.

"What's his problem now?" asked Jackson between thrusts. "I spit on it to make it easy for him."

"Ignore him. He loves it like the good faggot he is. Right, boy?"

Jim tried to answer, but could only sob with pain.

"Answer me, mutherfucker!"

"Yes, sir," came Jim's weak response.

Jackson leaned over and pulled hard on Jim's nuts, making him scream.

"See, Beltman. He can talk louder than that. Come on, boy, answer the nice officer like you mean it."

"Yes, sir!"

Beltman gave Jim the back of his hand. Jim cried out again as he tasted blood.

"Don't you yell at me, cocksucker."

"This boy," said Jackson as he continued pumping Jim's butt, "definitely needs to be punished. Long arm of the law and all that, right, buddy?"

"He sure does, buddy. And we'll be happy to oblige him, won't we?"

"Fuck, yeah!"

Whether Jackson's enthusiasm was for punishing Jim or for spilling the contents of his bull sized balls into Jim's asshole, or both, Jim couldn't tell. He felt the man's load shoot inside his guts, pumping jism until it dripped onto the carpet.

Pulling out of Jim's hole, Officer Jackson commented on Jim's hesitation in obeying orders and noted that perhaps Jim didn't deserve good cop dick anyway. Officer Beltman agreed, but added that Jim still needed to be punished. Maybe then he'd be more grateful.

Too shocked to resist, Jim let himself be dragged into the bedroom, still in handcuffs. There he was gagged and whipped with a heavy belt (Jim's own), the two officers taking turns. When they'd finished, Jim only wavered near consciousness until he noticed a wetness in his crotch. He'd cum while they whipped him.

"Don't know why you want him for a slave, Beltman," Jackson was saying. "The boy's got no life in him."

"He's a natural. I could tell right away. Better than that cocksucking Danvers. Danvers keeps thinking he has rights. That's not what I want in a slave."

"He's a good cop, though," offered Jackson.

"But a better cocksucker."

The men laughed, remembering past exploits.

"Hey, I'm hard again, Beltman. What you say we use it again?"

"Good idea."

The men unzipped their pants again and took turn fucking Jim's ass, each cumming quickly to Jim's relief. When they were ready to go, Jackson asked Beltman if he didn't need his handcuffs.

"Almost forgot. Thanks."

He returned to the room where they'd left Jim and removed the handcuffs.

"Okay, piggy, you can go about your business now. I'll be back to see you again soon. Just be ready for me, next time."

Jim heard the motorcycles drive off and fell asleep where they'd left him in a pile on the floor.

"Sure, it sounds hot," said Gene. "But did you enjoy it?"

They were sitting over beers at the Eagle early on a weekday evening. Jim had told Gene about Beltman and Jackson's visit.

"I must've liked it. I came without touching myself."

"But they hurt you."

"So?"

Gene laughed but got serious again.

"No, Jim. That's not what I meant. They weren't sadistic, you know? Just mean. I don't like that. Not for you."

Jim scowled.

"Don't be a hypocrite. You like it well enough when you're getting it nice and nasty. I should know if anyone does."

"That's not what I'm talking about. What we do is different. You're talking about brutality for its own sake. That's dangerous. And ask yourself this: Why has no one ever heard of this Beltman guy? I'll tell you, Jim. Because he's dangerous and knows enough to keep to himself."

Jim was obstinate. "But he was with Royal Jackson, and everyone knows him. He's a good guy."

"I guess. Except he keeps Alan almost naked, even during the winter."

"May Alan *likes* it," asserted Jim. "Maybe *I* like how these guys did me."

There was a sudden pause.

"You're telling me to mind my own business, aren't you?"

"Isn't the first time."

Gene suggested another beer. Not much of a drinker, though, the more Jim drank, the more hostile he became.

"Besides Gene, look at the men you turn me on to. Like that guy you and I were supposed to play with? What ever happened to him? Last time anyone saw him was that night he stood us up and disappeared down Folsom Street on the end of a leash."

Furious, Gene threw a few bills on the bar and left without a word.

Beltman didn't bother to knock on his next visit. It was well pass midnight when he picked the lock open and burst into Jim's bedroom waving a flashlight in his victim's startled face. As soon as he realized it was Beltman, Jim scrambled out of bed and kneeled down to kiss the policeman's boots.

Beltman picked up the same heavy belt he'd used last time (set deliberately aside by Jim for the officer's convenience) and began to slowly whip Jim's ass, thighs, back and shoulders. He started easy this time, with quick deliberate flicks of the belt over the kneeling body. As Jim's body, still bruised from the last beating, grew accustomed to the pain, the pain increased, taking Jim further and further towards what he believed was his true self. When he at last became oblivious to the pain, and had reached that state of absolute trust, the whipping stopped.

Jim heard the booted feet walk to the bathroom, then the sound of running water. Jim smiled to himself, sure that Beltman was now bringing him a glass of water, an act of tenderness to balance the beating.

Suddenly the belt cut through the air like a sword. Where it had been doubled over before, Jim now received the full length of the belt, now wet with Beltman's piss. The leather cracked over Jim's already discolored flesh, cutting into it, leaving the residue of piss to seep into the cuts and intensify the pain. Jim let out a scream as he felt not only the torment of his body, but the shattering of that perfect trust he'd felt in Beltman only a moment before. With each new lash of the belt, Jim howled anew.

Just as suddenly, Beltman stopped.

"Wouldn't you know it. Now my dick's hard."

Jim barely heard him above the spasms of his own breathing. His body trembled as Beltman dropped his pants and kneeled behind him. Beltman's thick cock rammed between the raw ass cheeks with a single push. With a second push, the full length of it was buried inside him. Jim only gasped once at this new assault.

Beltman took his time, pumping with an even tempo until, closing in on his climax, he increased the pace to the fury of a battering ram. Jim cried out again, this time with pleasure, achieving his own climax.

When Beltman had finished and pulled out his dick, he kicked Jim over onto his side. Sweat had soaked through his uniform. He mopped his brow with his sleeve before pulling a collar, thick and heavy, out of his leather jacket. Pulling Jim's head up by his hair, he fastened the collar around Jim's neck. Jim felt the collar being put on him, heard the click of the padlock as the collar was put in place. His dick was hard again.

The following night Jim answered the door expecting Beltman and found Officer Danvers at his door instead. Danvers walked in and grabbed Jim without a word, handcuffing him and pushing him to the floor with a knee in his groin. Once on the floor, Danvers fucked his face without a word. This done, a leash was attached to Jim's collar and Jim was taken into a waiting patrol car and thrown in the back seat.

Moments later they stopped at a darkened side street where Jim was blindfolded. Another man, another patrolman Jim assumed, joined him in the back seat to fuck his face. Even blindfolded Jim recognized the girth of Officer Jackson's dick and the rhythm of the fuck.

Finally, after another short drive, he was pulled from the car and up some stairs, through a door, down a hall, and finally down another flight of stairs. Here he was stripped and the blindfold removed. His eyes adjusted to the darkness just quick enough to see that he'd been left in a barred cell with a toilet, sink, a bare mildewed mattress and a single army blanket. He turned at the sound of the cell door clanging shut just fast enough to see Danvers, Jackson and Beltman exit up the stairs. He could hear them laughing as they climbed the steps, then the sound of their heavy booted feet over his head, then nothing. Suddenly, all Gene had said made sense. For the first time since the adventure had begun, he grew afraid.

Jim was kept in his cell except when he was being used by Beltman or one of the other officers. Danvers was there whenever Beltman wasn't and fucked which ever orifice pleased him at the moment. He also fed and bathed Jim as he might have an animal whose owner was away. He never beat Jim as this privilege was reserved exclusively for Beltman. Jim never struggled against the beatings because he enjoyed them, achieving in each new assault new depths of pleasure, orgasms more intense than any he'd experienced before.

It was weeks before Jim realized (as Danvers was bathing him in a wash tub on the floor) that what bothered him most was not being held prisoner so much as not really wanting to escape even if he could. Jim was certain that Gene had looked in on him after their fight and, since he had a key, would take care of the cats and things until – until whatever happened happened.

One day another slave was brought by Officer Jackson, led down the stairs on a leash. Beltman opened the cage and the new comer scampered in obediently.

"Shall we leave them there while we go out a while?"

"Yeah. I heard somewhere that it's good for them to be left alone together."

"Shit."

The two slaves watched anxiously as the door closed at the top of the stairs.

"Alan!"

"Hiya, Jimbo."

They embraced.

"It feels so strange. I haven't been allowed to talk to anyone in so long."

"You're never let out?"

"No."

"Do you like it this way?"

"Not really. But if I ask him, he'll *never* let me out. He's like that."

Alan sat silent a moment before asking, "Do you *want* out?"

"Sometimes. I like being here, but I also miss my own place. I like being owned, but not by him. I don't like *him* at all. He's not the man I thought he was, not man enough to be tender."

"I never liked him," agreed Alan. "He's had lots of boys and they all leave him. That's why you don't get to go out. He's afraid you'll leave him too. The only one who didn't cut out on him is Danvers and he only stayed so Beltman who'd train him to be a master. That's why Danvers is the one who looks after you. Beltman needs a sitter and Danvers thinks he wants to be like Beltman."

"How do you know all this?"

"I listen; I hear things. I've got to or I wouldn't know what was going on half of the time. I sure can't ask. Is Beltman your first master?"

"Hardly. But I've never been kept prisoner like this before. It's so weird. And what's weirder is that a part of me likes it this way."

"Do you want out?"

"He won't let me out."

"That's not the question," asserted Alan. "Do you want out?"

There was a long pause as Jim grasped for an answer.

"I guess I won't know if I want to leave until I can leave," he said at last. "And if I do leave him, I must want something more than this after all."

Alan nodded.

They heard the door open at the top of the stairs.

"When you get a chance," whispered Jim hurriedly. "Tell Gene where I am, okay?"

Alan nodded again.

Jim was fed and bathed as usual by Officer Danvers. Nothing hinted that anything was at all different until Danvers pulled out a pair of barber's clippers and trimmed Jim's hair and beard to a uniform quarter-inch all over. Jim hadn't looked in a mirror in weeks and wondered what he looked like. He was sure he'd grown thinner but hoped the simple calisthenics he'd done in his cage had been enough to keep his body toned.

After Danvers had finished grooming Jim, he tossed a pair of leather briefs at him and told him to put them on with his boots. Officer Beltman arrived to inspect Danvers' handiwork and with a grunt of approval took the leash and led Jim up the stairs.

When they reached the sidewalk, Jim was told to walk three steps behind Beltman. It was dark now and chilly, even without the usual fog. Jim was unaware of this, however, as he looked at the surrounding neighborhood, figuring out exactly where South of Market he'd been kept. Beltman pulled on his leash and barked an order, telling Jim to keep his eyes lowered to the dog shit on the sidewalk at all times.

When they got to the Brig, Jim was ordered to walk ahead to make a way through the crowd for his master. They approached the bar and a stool was immediately cleared for them. Jim was chained to the stool and ordered to sit on the floor. He obeyed and found Alan next to him, also tethered to a bar stool. They nodded to one another but said nothing. They stayed silent for over an hour, exchanging occasional glances and listening intently to what was being said above them. Finally Officer Jackson gave them permission to talk between themselves.

"What would they have to say to each other?" asked Beltman.

"Not much, but they've been such good boys."

Jim and Alan spoke quietly on the floor, each with an ear cocked for his master's voice in case something was suddenly demanded of him.

"Have you decided anything?" asked Alan.

"No."

"You could leave now, you know."

"I wouldn't know where to go."

"Your place is still there, Jim. Gene's taking care of it. And he called your office with some excuse. I talked to him."

Jim nodded, a little surprised by Gene's thoroughness..

"He's been asking around about you," Alan continued, reading Jim's face. "It's a really a small town, you know. Anyway, Gene wanted to know where you were so I told him."

"But –."

"He said not to worry."

"About what?"

"I thought you'd know. He just said not to worry."

Later that night Jim was taken to the Slot and put on display, whipped severely for the pleasure it gave Beltman, then restrained in a sling and left for all to use. A hood was put over his head with holes only for the lips and nose, providing access to his mouth not only as a hole to fuck, but a place to pee in.

Jim stayed in the sling for hours, his bladder filled with other men's piss and his bowels with their cum. Finally he was released and a allowed to curl up on the floor with a bowl of water beside him. Jim fell into a deep sleep at once and, unable to control it any longer, peed all over himself as he slept. Even so, his dreams were pleasant ones.

He was woken with a nudge of someone's foot.

"Time to go, mister."

"Sir?"

"No more guys left to play with. Go on home now."

"Sir?"

The hood was unfastened and pulled off of his head. Jim blinked in the strange brightness of the morning light. A stranger was kneeling next to him.

"Time to go," the stranger said again.

"Where's my master?"

"No master here," said the man. "Go on home."

"My master brought me. Did he leave me here? Was there a message?"

"Sorry, kid. He probably got loaded and went home. You better go find him."

Then, seeing the state of filth Jim was in, the stranger suggested Jim shower first. Jim declined and at once stumbled into the brightness of the morning in his leather briefs, collar and boots. He wandered down Folsom Street with his leash in his mouth and the hood clenched in his fist. He was tripping down Seventh Street, oblivious to the stares and cat calls he attracted, when a patrol care pulled along beside him.

"Master?"

It was Officer Jackson, looking grim and motioning Jim into the car.

"I've been looking all over for you. Checked out the Slot and they said I just missed you. You've been there all this time?"

"Yes, sir. I fell asleep."

They drove in silence a while. When the car stopped, they were in front of Jim's home. Jim panicked.

"Why are you bringing me here?"

"It's your home, ain't it?"

"Not anymore. I want my cell. Where's my master? Where's Officer Beltman?"

"Things have changed," said Jackson. "You're free now. Go on in."

"What's going on?" asked Jim. Why won't you take me home? Does he have a new slave. If he does I'll –."

"Not hardly, boy, not hardly," the policeman chuckled.

Jackson put the car in gear.

Jim saw the outside of Beltman's house for the first time in daylight. Stuck between two warehouses in an alley beneath a freeway overpass, the old wood rotted at the foundation and the paint, once a bright yellow, had peeled off much of the house. Jim wondered at how comfortable it had been while he had lived there in his cage in the basement.

Jackson led him through the front door and down the back steps to the room that had been Jim's home all those weeks. Stunned by what he saw, Jim was unable to move, unable to speak for some time. When he did come out of his shock, it was anger, overwhelming rage, mounting inside of him and waiting to explode.

Danvers was laying back in an easy chair smoking a cigar as half a dozen policeman took turns fucking Officer Beltman. Beltman lay prone in the sling, once Jim's exclusive province. The men pumped the officer's butt, each with his own unique fury, each taking vengeance on the man who had once been his master.

"Jackson, you're back! And Jimmy, too," said Danvers. "Glad you could make it. Now we're all here, Beltman's first slave – Officer Jackson – and his last." He made a motion towards Jim. He sucked on his cigar and gave a great laugh. "You see, Jimmy, Beltman's enslaved and fucked his last man. I made him into what he was always afraid to be: A fuck-slave, a lousy cocksucking faggot. All that macho bullshit he laid on us. He couldn't even hold onto a slave 'cause he either half-killed them or they saw through him and knew what a wimp he really was."

Jim approached the sling. Jackson's firm hand rested on his shoulder, either to comfort Jim at the shock of seeing Beltman so abused, or perhaps to steady himself. Jim didn't notice either way. The rage inside him rose to a head as he watched the last policeman pull out his spent dick while Beltman begged for more.

"How'd you do it?" asked Jim, already knowing why, even if Danvers hadn't explained it for him. "How did you get him like this?"

"Some guys thought we should drug him, but I said it wouldn't mean anything then. No, I wanted him to beg for it and know what he was doing. So last night we grabbed him, tied him down in one of the rooms and locked the door. We just pulled out our dicks and waited after that. You should've heard him screaming, telling us we were gonna get pulled off of the force when he got through with us. But we didn't say nothing to him, just kept pulling on our dicks 'cause we could see he was really hungry for it. It was in his eyes, see, like a dog that hasn't been fed for a while. Then he cracks and we hear this little voice come out of the big macho cop that sounds more like a little kid than a *police officer*." He threw a sneer in Beltman's direction. "And you know what he says? 'Please.' That's all, just 'Please'."

"Then you fucked him?"

"Naw. That wasn't enough to suit me. I waited until he started sobbing, begging for dick, for *cop* dick. Isn't that right, boy?"

Danvers barked the last question at their former master who answered in a thin whiny voice that Jim had never heard before.

"Yes, sir. Please, sir. Fuck me some more, sir. Either end, sir. Please, could I have some more dick, sir? Some cop dick, sir? Please, sir? Please..."

Jim felt a turning in his stomach as his rage came to a peak. He pulled down the leather briefs he still wore and forced his dick into Beltman's mouth, forced it down the policeman's throat in fast, deep thrusts, trying to choke him, or even hurt him. He came too quickly, pouring out his cum into Beltman's eager mouth.

"Now we've all had him," said Danvers. "What do we do with him?"

"He's your responsibility, now," said Jim. "Keep him. That is, if you can handle the responsibility of taking care of a dog. If not, put him out of his misery."

Jim looked at Beltman as he said this and saw the man's eyes glaze over, as if for some unattainable longing, one Jim hoped had no name.

Jackson unlocked the collar on Jim's neck and took him upstairs where he could shower and put on some clean clothes. He offered to drive Jim home in the patrol car, but Jim demurred.

Jim took a final glance into the basement room and saw Beltman moving about on his knees, his great muscled frame in chains. He crawled from man to man, sucking this one's dick, drinking that one's piss, putting out his tongue to receive the ashes from another man's cigar, licking the boots of another.

"I don't know," said one of the men. "What do we do with him now?"

"The kid was right," said another.

"Naw," said a third. "We can share him, take turns feeding him and stuff."

"Maybe..." said the first cop.

Jim closed the door and walked the few blocks home.

Gene was waiting on his doorstep.

"Hi, Jimbo. Just got done feeding your cats. They've missed you."

Jim smiled at his best friend.

"Thanks."

"And I missed you, too."

They embraced.

"But listen, Jimbo. You be careful. Next time I might not be able to fix things so –."

"What?"

"Never mind," Gene laughed unconvincingly. "Just kidding." He opened the door to the upstairs flat where he lived above Jim. "Come on up. I'll fix us some lunch."

Jim followed wordlessly, thinking that he really did miss his cats.

UNNATURAL SONG

Is it possible that you are the one, here at last:
The one who will appease my savage longing?

-Frank Wedekind

When Royal left Alan for Willy-Boy, saying that Will was the better bottom, the more obedient slave, Alan shaved off his beard. It had been as blond as the rest of him but very full, giving him the appearance of a bantam-weight Viking. He also got a new apartment, a new phone number, and left no forwarding address. With the beard gone no one, at least initially, would know who Alan was, that he'd been Officer Royal Jackson's boy for something like seven years. Now he was nobody, another face on Folsom Street, another slave without a master.

For months he had stayed a recluse, leaving his Potrero Hill apartment only for work or groceries. But in the end the need to be with another man, the need for more sensation than his own hands could provide, overwhelmed him.

He put on his leather and mounted his bike. He felt naked, vulnerable, without a collar around his neck and a master by his side. He was afraid being out on his own for the first time, but the need to find himself again in subservience was stronger than his fear.

It was already late. Men were milling about the doors of bars eyeing each other cautiously, looking hopefully at the fleeting figure of Alan flying down the street on his bike. He stopped near Rogers Street and wondered if he could crash the orgy he knew was happening in a warehouse at the alley's end. Men paraded past him, guarded in their leathers.

Alan contemplated going into the bar on the corner but it was already after one o'clock, he told himself, and the best men had already been taken. This was only an excuse, of course. He was really afraid of seeing Royal – or being seen by him. He thoughtfully stroked the new stubbled smoothness of his face, not moving.

Alan turned around towards the bar and saw Royal coming down the street in his leather, looking like chiseled onyx, his face almost as black as the leather. Following behind him on a leash was Will, naked but for leather briefs, low boots, and the wide, heavy dog collar Royal insisted he wear. Will's hands were bound in front of him, his head bent down. Alan felt a rush of adrenaline, the fear and anger struggling within him. With screeching tires he began a random journey through the network of alleys that laced through the neighborhood: Hattie, Natoma, Langton, Harriet, Shotwell, Rausch... He drove for hours, never stopping, hardly slowing down except to avoid an accident. Then he stopped for no apparent reason, as suddenly as he had started, in a nameless dilapidated alley off of Eighth Street.

He sat for a time on his bike, looking blankly into the darkness of the alley. He heard footsteps in the stillness. Steps that belonged to a man, he was certain, falling softly on the littered pavement. Alan sat still. There was a single street lamp shining across Eighth Street. The only other light was from the headlight of his bike. Alan waited for the man to show himself, poised for whatever came.

Then he appeared from somewhere within the shadows, unearthly, and to Alan's mind, breathtaking: an unnatural beauty that horrified and attracted. His hair and beard showed auburn even in the dim light. He was smaller than Royal, Alan noted (but Royal was a very big man) though still taller than Alan by half a head. Where Royal's skin was a deep chocolate, this man was uncommonly pale. His entire being spoke power in a way that Alan had never known before. Royal had embellished himself with the trappings of power – the uniform he wore as a policeman, the symbols of servitude that he insisted Alan (and now Will) wear – but this man, this pale, unearthly stranger in the pre-dawn shadows, *was* power. He was encased in leather. As others seem born to wear leather, this man seemed to have been born *in* it.

Alan's eyes were riveted to the stranger's. The man nodded and Alan returned the nod. For just a second it seemed that the man was about to speak to him, but then he looked up into the night sky, shook his head, and walked up the broken steps of an old, abandoned looking house. Alan could just make out the shadow of the man as he nodded to Alan again and disappeared into the deeper darkness of the house. Alan held his breath and waited for the man to do or say something. Nothing. Alan felt something had happened, though, that the man had told him to come again, that Alan was welcome – even wanted.

Alan sat motionless for some time. Then, sensing the approach of morning, he quietly coasted his bike down Eighth Street before starting it. He didn't wish to disturb his new master with the harsh sound that starting the bike would make.

Alan woke with a start, his heart pounding. He thought someone had called him. He listened but heard nothing. Then the sound of someone whistling, eerie and tuneless.

Alan got out of bed and walked, still naked, to the window that looked over his neighbor's backyard. There he was, a statue in the moonlight, whistling his unnatural song. Alan opened the window and leaned over the sill, felt the light summer fog cling to the air around him. He breathed it in, cool and sharp, wondering at the dream he assumed this to be. Suddenly, with a single, effortless leap, the man was at the window, balanced delicately on the narrow ledge, looking deep into Alan's eyes. Alan stepped back, afraid, looking about his Spartan bedroom for some sort of weapon.

As swiftly and silently as he had jumped to Alan's window, the man was now in Alan's bedroom.

"I've come for you."

"Now?"

The man's green, almost feline eyes, locked onto Alan's. His boots fell silently on the bare floor as he came towards Alan.

"Now."

Alan froze, immobile with equal parts fear and desire. He waited for the man's touch, for the power he hoped would subdue and comfort him.

"My name is Nachman."

"Sir."

A gloved hand reached out, ever so gently. Alan caught his breath in short gasps. His cock twitched. Alan opened his mouth and offered it to Nachman as a gift, hoping it would be kissed, or fucked. Nachman's hand softly caressed Alan's face, his strange green eyes fixed on his quarry. Alan's cock twitched again, exploding over Nachman's leathers, shooting cum in long, agonizing spasms.

Alan fell to his knees, trembling, his breathing shallow and rapid, as if he'd been suffocated. Without a word he knew what to do. He licked the leather clean, covering every bit of it with his tongue, relishing the cum because it had touched his master's leather and was therefore sacred.

When he'd finished, Alan again looked up into the lunar green eyes. Nachman reached down to Alan, and touched him with the same gentleness as before, with the same gloved hand.

Alan slept feverishly for nights to come, always dreaming of Nachman. His waking hours had a dream like quality. As if drugged, he'd stare into space for hours. If he let his awareness flow unguided he saw Nachman clearly. Only when he tried to see Nachman's face did it disappear, hover just out of sight, haunting him with unrealized desires.

Unable to sleep, Alan wandered the maze of streets and alleys of the warehouse district, always without direction, but always avoiding that one dark alley where he first saw Nachman. He was afraid of the alley, afraid to see Nachman, afraid that Nachman wouldn't be there, and afraid that what he insisted to himself was a dream might prove to be just that.

The fever of his nights increased. The dreams of Nachman invaded even his waking hours. He collapsed exhausted at work one day and went home ill. He tried to sleep but his rest was fitful; his dreams woke him. He walked the streets again. Too weak to resist, he let himself be drawn, as if pulled in by an unseen tide, towards the alley.

It was well past midnight. Even in the darkness, the nameless alley opened up to him like a cavern, a gaping maw prepared to swallow him whole. He came to the house, saw the unlit windows and shadows that crossed them like layers of darkness.

Something inside him rebelled, perhaps the last shred of sanity or an instinct for survival. Reason told him that his obsession was nonsense, that he was a victim of his own weakness, suffering in the aftermath of Royal's desertion. Bolstered by this insight, he turned to go only to discover that he was already on the front porch of the house, though he had no memory of walking up the stairs. He felt a chill rush through him. Reason evaporated.

He turned back to the door and found it open. He went in, stumbled about in the cluttered darkness until he discovered the staircase. A slow ascent. Above him was Nachman's face, almost luminescent, mirroring the light of his eyes.

"Alan."

"Master, I've come."

"I've waited for you too long."

"Forgive me, sir. I mistook you for a dream."

Alan stood before him, waiting. He felt as if his name had been spoken again, though he'd heard nothing, and raised his eyes to meet his master's. He opened his mouth to scream but didn't. He saw Nachman's face clearly, saw the delicate, razor-like fangs, now so pronounced, that he'd not noticed before.

Alan gave into desire. The will to resist gave way and he pulled at the collar of his shirt to bare his throat. The sharp fangs sliced easily, almost imperceptibly, through Alan's flesh. Alan felt his cock stiffen as his life was sucked out of him, felt it explode.

Strangely, it was only now that the fever passed, that he was able to live from day to day as others did, to sleep deeply at night unburdened by dreams. He caressed the thin wounds healing on his neck, feeling when he did an overwhelming eroticism – even to the point of climax, followed by a sense of peace that held him in trance.

As Alan went about his daily life, he was comforted by the thought that Nachman was sleeping and dreaming of him. Nights and days passed faster than he'd ever imagined they could before Nachman took him. His hunger was now satisfied, his passion quenched. Nachman's presence no longer haunted him. It was now a benevolent omnipresence whispering in the heart's darkest corners. For now he renewed the supply of blood for his beloved. When ready, he'd be called again.

One night he heard Nachman's whistle while he slept and followed it without waking. He found Nachman waiting in the shadows of a crowded street. Alan watched (seeing him clearly but knowing that others could not see him) as Nachman slipped unnoticed through the door of a bar. Then, as if Nachman was suddenly visible, Alan saw nervous young men approach his master with offers of complete submission. Nachman caressed one such boy, one younger and softer than Alan, touched him gently as if consuming the boy's earthly beauty. Nachman brushed his lips against his victim's, then, pretended to caress the boy's throat with an open mouth. There was a single gasp, the briefest struggle, before the boy fell forward into Nachman's arms where he was held, comforted, as he died.

After Nachman had fed, he left the boy, barely breathing, slumped over a bar stool. No one noticed, thinking only that the boy was drunk.

Alan heard the whistling a second time. He woke up and without pausing went to open his bedroom window. The fog was thick, even for summer. There was no moonlight to see by, but Alan knew Nachman was there. He paused to breathe in the night air before calling softly, "Nachman."

Nachman was at the window, then in the room. He cupped Alan's face gently in his gloved hands and kissed him softly. "Did you see?"

"Yes!"

Nachman kissed Alan again. His lips were colder now, having lost the warmth of the kill. He caressed Alan's throat where he had once taken drink. Alan's whole body stiffened. He ejaculated, struggled to catch his breath. Without a word Nachman disappeared through the window.

Royal had had a way of giving orders, leaving written instructions for Alan to read and obey. Alan had thought this constant attention to his subservience ideal. Both men had taken their roles seriously and Alan had thrived under the constant duress of the relationship. But while he felt objectified by Royal, Alan now realized, he never felt completely possessed by him, never felt owned out right because Royal neglected to take care of what he owned. Alan had been expected to take care of his own needs as well as Royal's. Any pleasure Alan got (which had been considerable, after all) had been incidental as far Royal was concerned.

With Nachman, Alan felt completely at one with his passions. Nachman's pleasure in him was explicit and fed Alan's sense of worth. Nachman owned Alan body and soul, there was no question, but loved him as well. Whatever longings Alan may have had for Royal's cruel touch now dissolved in the intensity of his need to be nothing more than the object of Nachman's desire. In all of this, Alan found peace.

Each evening Alan walked the shabby streets to Nachman's house. The sun set as Alan climbed the stairs to the vault like room where Nachman slept, greeting him as he emerged from one darkness into another. Nachman's tenderness towards Alan at these moments left Alan trembling and as exhausted as if he'd been taken.

On the nights when Alan was taken, Nachman's tenderness gave way to lust and hunger. He bared his teeth as Alan approached, his eyes glowing. Alan's cock would harden, then, as Nachman's delicate razor teeth sank quickly into his throat, Alan would feel the rush of orgasm.

Alan stopped passing out when Nachman fed. Each time he found himself stronger than the last. Before the summer ended, Alan was changing into something more than what he had been. What had been surreal now seemed natural while his previous existence took on a quality of a half-remembered dream. Always pale, Alan took to avoiding the sun altogether and found comfort in the City's seasonal fog. His skin was now translucent and friends thought him strangely ill.

One evening he arrived at Nachman's home to find his master already sitting in the lower chamber of the house. He kneeled at Nachman's feet, kissed his gloved hand and waited in silence. In time, Nachman spoke. His voice was grave, almost sad. Alan saw the lines of melancholy drawn across the usually handsome face, a face that remembered much.

"When my master made me centuries ago, I was not much older than you, Alan. He loved me and wanted me forever. I thought he was the devil at first – people still believed in the devil then – and tried to escape. I was not so willing to love as I am today."

Very gently he stroked Alan's hair. Alan felt a shiver of pleasure.

"I can make you like me, but most people are too weak to thrive in the darkness as we do. They grow weak, become unhappy until they despair and end their lives. They stop feeding and disappear. My master told me that only those who see us when we wish to be shadows can share our life. You are one of those people, Alan. When I saw you that night, saw you watching me, I knew... And I've loved you, wanted you since then. So I looked for you, called you. Remember? You, my love, can live forever. You will grow strong as me one day. In time, you will be your own master, but there will centuries devoted to me before then. I love you, Alan, and must possess you."

Alan was silent, overcome.

Quietly Nachman took Alan's hand and led him up the stairs and into the chamber where he slept. At last, thought Alan, it is happening.

In the still, lightless chamber was a simple slab of marble on a pedestal. At regular intervals were large brass rings.

Alan undressed and laid down on the marble platform as he was told, his cock arching upward in the still, musty air. Alan felt his arms and legs being secured to the brass shackles, his body stretched across the length of the marble slab. He waited in the dark, breathless in his excitement, but unafraid.

A candle was lit and Alan watched Nachman pass a needle through the flame. Alan understood at once. Sweat ran over him as his excitement increased. His cock, turgid and swollen bounced into empty space.

"I'm marking you as mine, as my slave so all men will know."

Nachman held Alan's nipple in one hand and pushed the needle through Alan's flesh. Before Alan's first cry subsided, Nachman passed the needle through the second nipple and the urethra. Alan sobbed gently as gold rings were slid into place. He felt a warm trickle of blood run down his body, then Nachman's cold tongue licking cat-like at the red rivulets. Pleasure became pain as Alan's body convulsed, his cock shooting cum until his balls were shriveled and empty.

Alan was given the pleasure of the hunt.

There was no shortage of prey. Alan's eyes had hardened and his face now showed a purpose that attracted eager submissives who thought him the master. Haunting alleys and bars, waiting in the shadows for the right man to approach him, Alan proudly bared the gold rings in his nipples, arousing admiration and desire in the men who approached him.

The victims were brought to the house. Alan used the same story again and again: "My lover's at home, but I know a place where we can get it on."

Lighting a candle, Alan would lead the man up the dark stairs into Nachman's vaulted lair. There the unsuspecting man was taken. Alan watched each feeding with eagerness, stroking his cock at the sight of Nachman's eyes glowing in the dark, at the small cry each victim made, the inevitable but futile struggle as Nachman's teeth sliced through the throat. When the body dropped to the floor, Nachman would gaze deeply into Alan's eyes, blood dripping from his mouth and eagerly retrieved by the tongue. Then Alan would shoot, covering the corpse with cum.

One night, as the victim still struggled to live, still fought for breath, Nachman interrupted his feast to say, "Now you feed. It's time to taste what you hunt so well."

Alan didn't hesitate. Blood, he discovered, was not unlike cum, warm and sweet with life. When he had fed and the body slumped to the floor, Nachman finished by feeding on Alan.

Alan reached a new euphoria in this, feeding and being fed upon. He felt drugged, only cleaner, richer. That day he slept in Nachman's arms.

"You choose them so well, Alan. You choose those I'd have chosen myself."

Nachman spoke gently, stroking Alan's hair. They had just fed and were filled with the warm lethargy that followed drinking blood. There was no need for Alan to hurry to respond. Just as the elderly will speak their minds because they see the moment as immediate and not to be wasted, so Alan and Nachman took their time when they spoke because they had the leisure (all eternity) to do so.

"I pick those I think closest to perfect," said Alan in time. "Men so beautiful I'd hate to see them whither and grow old. They're too handsome to fade without bringing me pain." Nachman leaned over from where he sat in his chair and kissed Alan on the lips.

For weeks now Alan had fed only on blood, his nights spent serving Nachman, his days sleeping in his lover's arms. His job and friends were a vague memory now, almost forgotten. He'd become an enigma. Only those who got glimpses of him hunting even knew he was still alive.

When Alan awoke, Nachman had already risen.

"Tonight," said Nachman.

He grabbed Alan's face and kissed him. His mouth felt icy against Alan's warmth. His fangs cut into the flesh of Alan's mouth as his tongue lapped up the blood.

"There is no choice but to obey you."

They hunted that night and fed together, but when they'd finished, instead of Nachman feeding on Alan, Alan fed on him. There was a shared euphoria in the feeding. Both orgasmed, shooting blood instead of semen, blood they licked hungrily from each other's cocks. Alan smiled, licked his lips, when they were done and discovered that his canines were now longer, sharper. They'd grown to fangs so quickly.

The night opened up to Alan. It was if he had suddenly been given the gift of sight. Colors were now vivid in the darkness where once there had only been shades of gray. When he and Nachman hunted together, sharing the kill, it seemed to Alan that they fed not so much on their victims' blood as on their beauty, consuming not their lives but their essences. Time lost all meaning. Seasons passed and meant little more to Alan than the vague discomfort of being wet in winter or the inconvenience of shorter summer nights.

The passion between Alan and Nachman increased. They made love by sharing their victims' blood, by reveling in the beauty of those they fed upon. Long hours were spent talking. Lonely for centuries, Nachman shared his life with Alan, recounted the endless episodes that had made up the years of his unnatural existence. Alan listened silently, in constant awe of the numberless nights Nachman had lived, never tiring of Nachman's voice.

Alan learned to move with the deftness of a shadow, to disappear into the mist that hung over the City. He felt at one with the fog, with the endless possibilities that the night unfolded to him.

They prepared to travel. Nachman wanted to show Alan the world he had lived in years before, for Alan to meet others like themselves. Arrangements were made, elaborate but necessary to keep themselves from daylight. Endless attention was paid to time tables so that they would both leave and arrive in darkness.

Not long before they were to leave, Alan went walking alone, keeping himself a shadow in the streets. He had already fed with Nachman, but now he hungered for a memory he couldn't place. He wandered through the streets that years before had been his refuge and solace. Suddenly he was lurched from the seclusion of his thoughts at the sound of his name.

"Alan! Where've you been?"

Alan looked at the man, wearing only jeans and boots in the mild autumn night. A length of chain was secured about his neck, fastened with a lock. Alan recognized it, remembered that the collar had once been his.

"Will."

"We all thought you'd died or something. No one's seen you in years. Are you still upset about Royal?"

"Royal? No..." Alan answered vaguely. He looked about him and realized that he was on Harrison Street, not far from the Eagle. Others might come along and he didn't want to be seen, better the world did think him dead. He also realized that Will had seen him while he had meant to be a shadow. Feeling suddenly more human, he covered his anxiety with a smile. "I have a new lover, now. I'm happier than I ever was with Royal. You're still his slave? Where are you living these days?"

"Same place on Isis. How long has it been, Alan? Wait 'til I tell the guys!"

"A year at least..."

"Hah! More like five! Why don't you come for a drink? The bars close in an hour and Royal's on duty 'til four. Come on."

"No, but thanks, Will. I'm meeting my lover soon. He's expecting me."

"Okay, but call me. Okay? I can't wait to tell the others!"

Some trace of human emotion had remained in Alan, something like jealousy, a residual malice towards Will over Royal. It was simply self-preservation, he told himself. He would not let Nachman see Will (or be seen by him while Nachman was a shadow) for fear that Nachman would want Will as well. Alan would allow no room for competition, at least not yet. And never Will.

He followed Will home, sticking to the darkest shadows, treading silently across the narrow street. Leaping to the second story window, he watched, still a shadow to the world, as Will fell asleep. And waited.

Royal returned home in his squad car. He came in, stripped, and woke Will by fucking him, whipping Will's ass with his belt until it bled. The fuck lasted half an hour. Alan smelled the blood, looked anxiously at the still dark sky, but stayed where he was. Finally, the two lovers, master and slave, lay asleep in each others' arms.

With feline stealth, Alan slid the window open and stepped silently into the room. He stood motionless a moment, listening to the gentle even sound of the men's breathing, before approaching the bed.

He bent over them and saw the smaller, fairer figure of Will in Royal's immense brown arms. He saw the contrast with detachment of an aesthete and thought it beautiful. Very quietly he leaned down and bit into Will's neck, feeding until Will's heart stopped beating. When he'd finished, he continued looking at the clinging figures a while, wondering why, now that it was over, it had been so urgent that he feed on one man and not the other. He recognized them both, of course, knew that he had known them once, but their importance to him was now only a vague memory and difficult to account for.

The change in Alan was now complete. With Will had died the last of what had been human in Alan.

Nachman and Alan left soon after that. The old house in the alley off of Eighth Street stands empty today.

THE CIRCLE IS COMPLETE

Now we can cross the shifting sands.

- L. Frank Baum's last words

It all comes from the inside. It has to.

Really good actors can fill an empty stage with atmosphere. Props are superfluous. That's how I feel about being a master. A few hooks on the wall and a chair are all I need for my slave to be groveling at my feet begging for permission to breath. Elaborate playrooms are for those queens who "just *love* Victorianiana." The setting becomes more important than the drama and the actors get lost in the scenery.

I like to keep it simple. It's how I do everything.

The invitation was simple enough and that attracted me to the party in the first place: A plain white card in heavy stock where a vertical hand had written:

YOU'RE WANTED

Saturday, 7 April

10:00 to 2:00 PM

Our place.

Be there!

And it gave an address on Diamond Street

I liked their style, whoever *they* were. But I didn't know who it was from. I called an old friend who seemed to know everybody and asked him who lived at the address.

"Wish I knew. You know the place, though. It's that big, dark Victorian set behind a front yard filled with trees. I've heard that it's huge inside, much bigger than it looks from the front."

"Yeah, but who lives there?"

"No one's ever told me that."

Fucking dizzy queens.

So I went to check out the house myself. Sure enough, it was a dark Victorian set behind a high fence and a clump of trees. I walked along the length of the fence hoping to get a glimpse of someone or something that would tell me whose party I've been invited to. I could see that the yard had been more or less kept up, but not used. The trees had been allowed to grow dense enough to hide the second and third stories of the house.

The house was not inviting. It looked neither lived-in nor abandoned, but had the vacant look of a house between occupants.

I walked by the place whenever I could, even if it wasn't really on the way to anywhere. I'd walk the few extra blocks hoping to get a glimpse of more than the occasional light burning late at night. Then, just as suddenly, I gave up on it, decided not to go to the party, and forgot about the invitation. It wasn't until I was shuffling through some papers on my desk the afternoon before the party that I remembered it again. I found the invitation and studied the controlled even hand that had written it on the plane white stock.

I changed my mind a second time and decided to go. There was something in the handwriting that I wanted to know.

Since I didn't know who invited me, I wasn't sure what to expect. It might be purely social, or maybe an orgy. Al right, I'd come dressed for both. I put on a pair of leather jeans, a CHP shirt and a leather tie, a pair of boots and a black hankie tucked into my left hip pocket, the edge showing just enough to suggest the evil that lurked within. If the party did turn out to be an orgy, I figured my belt and the handcuffs hanging on the left epaulet of my motorcycle jacket would suffice for toys. Like I said at the beginning, I like to keep it simple.

The gate was wide open when I got there, and the short path to the door was lit with paper lanterns lining the walk. As I approached a cluster of people were being greeted by a woman with flaming red hair, milky white skin, and a black satin dress that clung to an otherwise naked body beneath. Besides the dress, she wore only a pair of menacing black stiletto heels.

The shoes were my clue that I was at the right party.

She extended her hand and said, "Hi. I'm Blade."

"I'm Steve," I explained and reached in my pocket for the invitation.

"Of course," she said recognizing me. "You're Gene's master. Come on in. I'll find Jack for you."

She turned on the point of her heel and walked down the hall into the front room where she cut a path through the people. She pointed a chair in one corner piled with an assortment of leather jackets and suggested that I leave mine there with the others.

Then it all fell into place. I knew who she was and where I'd met her months before. I also remembered Jack.

I'd met them at a mixed SM party at the Catacombs the winter before. I'd taken Gene with me. He explained (much to my consternation) that he also like submitting to women, and he begged me to please lend him to Blade at some point during the party, if only for half an hour. I agreed, a little reluctantly at first, but when the time came for me to lay back for a while, I handed him over to her. She grabbed the bound slave by his hair, dragged him into the playroom, threw him on the floor and whipped the holy hell out of him as he groveled and licked the clips of her high heeled pumps.

"She's really something else, isn't she?" said a man standing next to me as I watched the scene.

"I'll say," I said, not bothering to look at him. "I just hope Gene's got something left for me when she's done with him."

"Gene? Don't worry about him. He can play all night and not wear himself out. But then he picks the best tops, too, doesn't he?"

I acknowledged what I supposed to be a compliment with a nod, even if the idea of a bottom picking me didn't sound quite right. I wanted to know why this stranger knew so much about *my* slave.

"I'm Jack, by the way," he said extending a hand.

"Steve," I said shaking his strong grip in my own. Then I looked at him, a stud if I ever saw one. He was a lean but not skinny man, with fine, finished looking features. His hair was dark, almost black, and while he was clean shaven, there was still the shadow of a beard clearly visible. The sort of face you couldn't kiss without feeling the stubble. The skin was uncommonly pale and his eyes a bright blue. There's something about blue eyes and black hair that starts my juices flowing every time.

I offered him a beer and we talked while Blade and Gene did their stuff. I had to admit, they were hot to watch.

When Blade returned Gene to me, he came crawling on his stomach and kissed my boot. She handed me the leash and I thanked her for going to the trouble to a beat a worthless slave like Gene, and offered her a drink. She demurred, whispered something to Jack and strutted back into the playroom, her copper hair flying.

I looked over at Jack as we sat down, then at Gene, still on his stomach, his lips on my boot.

"Where's my foot stool, boy?" I barked. At once he became one, his weight resting on all fours. Jack and I used him to rest our feet on.

"You've got a good boy, there," Jack said.

"He's learning," said. I don't like anyone praising my slave but me; it might give him a swollen head.

"Steve," he said. "I'd like to check you out some time."

I raised an eyebrow. I knew what he meant, but the exact nature of the game, i.e., who would be the top, was unclear. I was a topman and only a topman, and nothing about Jack suggested that he was interested in anything less than complete control.

"Sure, Jack. When the boy here is rested, we can work him over together. I always learn watching another top up close."

"That's not what I meant."

My face must have betrayed my bewilderment. Jack gave a quick glance down at Gene on all fours supporting our booted feet, then looked at me.

"We'll talk about it some other time," he said. He gave Gene an affectionate shove with his boot as he got up, clapped me on the shoulder with a powerful hand and said, "Good to meet you."

Then he left the party.

I figured he'd gotten my address from Tron, a fixture at the Catacombs. He knew everyone and was famous, if for nothing else, than a notorious lack of discretion with other peoples' names, numbers and addresses.

I followed Blade, people moving quickly aside for her as they would for any absolute authority. Out of nowhere, it seemed, she pulled Jack from the crowd.

"Glad you could make it," he said with his wicked smile as he shook my hand.

He had on a pair of beautifully tailored leather pants – fine, supple leather – tucked into high-laced riding boots. The belt was equally impressive, woven leather with a simple brass buckle. Each biceps wore similar braided band. In the heat of the crowded room, he'd not bothered to wear a shirt, showing instead his lean, muscular torso and broad hairy chest. He kept his gloves on, also a fine grade of leather and as supple as his own skin. His black hair had been slicked back. His recently shaven jaw already showed the blue/black of his beard.

His bright blue eyes were as piercing as a cat's and as naked in their assault: The unnerving penetration of desire tempered with reason. It was the face of a man who got what he wanted, the face of a conqueror.

"Thanks for inviting me."

"You should know a lot of people here from the Catacombs."

"Yes," I agreed a little nervously. "Of course."

"Good. Well, I want to talk to you later. Right now I've got be a host."

"Sure."

I looked around at the expanse of humanity filling the house: Women and men in leather, corsets, boots, high heels, capes, harnesses, rubber, uniforms, chains, dog collars and leashes. The variations were endless.

I stood alone for a while, surrounded by people but still alone as a man can be at a party. I thought some more about Jack and all I wanted to do to him. I rearranged my crotch and looked at the crowd. I saw people I knew, a few of my own boys among them. I wondered if they were his boys as well.

A Boner Book

Mixing with the crowd, I nodded to friends, but I was the proverbial boy whistling in the dark.

After a while, the party thinned out but showed no signs of stopping. I expected then that it would turn into an orgy and that my hosts were waiting for the crowd to dwindle down to a manageable, perhaps select, group. I wondered if I was going to be invited to be a part of it. Then I saw Jack coming toward me and something in his eyes said "yes."

Without a word, he put an arm around my shoulder and led me away from the front room and down a dimly lit hallway where guests were already collecting in twos, threes and fours, negotiating the party to come in huddled whispers. Passing a bedroom I saw a two men fucking with brutal insistence, striking each other with open hands in their frenzy. I was turned on by the eroticism in the air and moved my dick in my pants to accommodate a growing hard-on.

We went into a room at the end of the long hallway. The door shut behind us. The room was a study, shelves lined with books. I felt something go cold in my gut.

I looked into his face, cut like granite, the shadow of his beard clear even in the dim light of the room, his blue eyes darkened to indigo. His voice had turned as cold as his eyes. He smiled a smile that was cruel and indulgent all at once.

"Come here," he said with some finality.

I approached. He grabbed me by my hair and kissed me full on the mouth, his tongue probing the orifice, fucking it with his tongue. There was no mistaking what he meant with the kiss. It took possession of me, claimed me as his.

I tried to pull back, but was in a hold I couldn't break. As big as I am, as strong as I am, I thought we were at least evenly matched. But I was overwhelmed by him, unable to break free of his hold on me.

"Don't resist me, Steve. You'll only make it harder on yourself. You can't get away. You might as well agree to it now."

I continued struggling until I noticed how our cocks had rubbed together during the struggle. Both of us were hard. My body had betrayed me. I was turned on, without knowing it. Any purpose to the struggle was, for the moment, over. I submitted, dropped to my knees and mouthed his dick through the supple, glossy leather of his pants.

"Good boy, Steve. Good boy."

He took off the woven leather belt, made a loop through the buckle and put it over my head and around my neck. I bowed my head and accepted the mark of subservience.

He reached behind one of the books on the shelf and the next thing I knew a door opened above the floor molding of the wall, a hidden passage. Jack pulled on the leash, led me through the opened panel and up the stairs. The door shut automatically behind us.

"The builder of this house," he explained casually as we climbed the narrow stairs, "hid Chinese refugee workers after the railroads were built. He helped smuggle them up to Canada so they wouldn't be deported. It was California's own underground railroad, less known than the other but no less important."

I said nothing as I followed behind him, feeling the tug of the belt around my neck as he moved quickly ahead of me. Eventually we reached a room, musty and cold with an unfinished wooden floor, empty except for an old ringed post used perhaps a century before for tethering horses along a street. Jack continued speaking as he tied me to the post.

"I'm a writer like you, you know. Only I'm an historian specializing in nineteenth century California. Maybe you read my book? No?" He turned back to face me again. "Tell me, Steve, what's your specialty?

Being a master? You're no more a master than you are an adequate slave. You're less than a slave, how could you be a decent master?"

I was on all fours but rose to my knees in protest. I opened my mouth to tell the bastard off. The back of his hand threw me back to the floor. I lay there stunned as he cuffed my ankles and wrists together. A gag was shoved into my mouth. He spoke with the same even tone as before, like a teacher with a less than promising pupil.

"I know you didn't say anything, Steve, but you were about to and I hadn't given you permission to speak. I think it's best to stop problems before they happen. It's the only way to keep a worthless piece of shit like you in line."

I tied to escape as he spoke, pulling on the ringed post with all my strength. Before he disappeared, taking the only source of light with him, he turned to me and spoke again, almost gently this time.

"This isn't a punishment, Steve, just part of the training. The gag is your punishment. Even without it no one would hear you scream. Until tomorrow, then. Right now I have to return to my guests."

He came back the next day. I was shivering on the floor, my will broken in the long night, unable to move or see. I greeted my master whimpering my gratitude at his return.

I can't explain what happened that night. Something snapped inside of me. I felt that I'd lost my manhood as surely as if he'd cut off my balls and stuffed them up my ass. I had no will of my own. I was his now. It was as if he had taken something from me, and I wondered if he had taken it when he kissed me: It had been the kiss that had thrown the switch inside of me, that had made me his.

He removed the gag and restraints. Then I was led on my makeshift leash, like a dog, further up the stairs and into the heart of the house.

We passed a mirror covering a narrow wall in what seemed to be an anteroom. I caught a glimpse of myself in it, my hair and beard matted from the night spent in bondage, my eyes surrounded by shadows, a small bruise decorating one side of my face. I saw myself broken.

"I've something special in mind for you, Steve. You must understand that I'm doing you a favor, opening you up. You need to know something about yourself. Even Gene says so."

I stopped in my tracks and looked up at him.

"Yes, even Gene. And he thinks you're a good topman, Steve – considering how little you really know."

We walked up a final flight of stairs into an attic room that had been renovated into a playroom. I looked about the room a little in awe by all I saw: Whips, chains, a series of metal shackles attached to the unfinished walls. In the center of the room hung an elaborate sling.

Omigod, I thought, he's gonna fuck me.

No one ever fucked me, except once. It was the first time I'd gone to Folsom Street. The bastard who picked me up put me in handcuffs and threw me over the hood of a car before he tore a hole in back of my Levis and shoved his meat in without even spitting on it. Then he took me home, tied me up and left me in a cage for the weekend. When I finally escaped a few days later, my ass was a bloody mess inside and out. Then my buddy Pete told me that the bastard was a cop. That really scared the shit out of me. And no one had fucked me since.

Now here I was in a sling, tied down and helpless again. I was scared, real scared, sweating and shivering so much the sling was shaking. All the while, Jack pulled on his dick and laughed at me. I wondered if he was as crazy as that cop had been.

"Like I said, Steve, I'm doing you a favor," he said as he slapped his fat dick against my ass cheeks. "A mind is like a window, or even an asshole, worthless unless it can be opened. And *your* mind – well, we'll find out what's inside it, won't we?"

He smiled his wicked smile before throwing back his head and laughing like the devil.

When he'd finished laughing, he greased a finger and inserted it. I winced and involuntarily tightened my hole. He smacked my ass.

"That's no way to behave, Steve, not when I'm doing you a favor."

"Yes, sir."

I tired to loosen my sphincter muscles, muscles I'd been unaware of my whole life, muscles I'd had no control over until that moment. Finding them now, relaxing them for my master, gave me my first hint of what lay ahead. His finger massaged my prostate a while before being joined by a second. Then a third. It felt good now. A soft moan escaped me, a sound I didn't recognize at first as having come from me.

Then his dick was there. I opened my eyes and looked at the mirror above the sling: Jack's cock, thick, heavy and massive, it's head just within reach of my asshole. He didn't push, though. I had to reach out for it myself, suck it deep inside me. I opened my hole as best I could and swallowed the tip of the mushroom head.

"Please, master," I begged. "More. Give it all to me, sir. Please."

I continued begging as I grabbed the size of his cock with my hole. He only smiled at the sight of me whimpering and so demoralized. Then, when I'd swallowed the entire dick's head, he gasped, threw his head back and pushed.

Nothing had equipped me for the pain I felt at that moment, or for the euphoria that followed so quickly on it's heels. It was as if I'd been exposed to all the forces of nature, turned inside out, and tossed to the wind. I'd been sent deep inside the heart of the earth and left there in this sudden, hot, and painful oblivion. Every thrust of his cock became the pounding of the earth's primeval heart. My balls and guts were battered from within.

I screamed with all that was in me: "FUCK ME! FUCK ME TO DEATH OR DIE TRYING!"

That's when I came.

I was kept inside the house for several days, usually in bondage. I was flogged, pierced, fucked. It all seemed natural now, as natural as inflicting it on Gene and others had been. I became as self-centered as a cat, accepting the torment as a cat accepts pleasure, consuming all stimuli selfishly and without constraint.

I became myself, or at least a part of myself long denied.

When I was released, a gold ring flashed from each nipple. One ring, Jack explained, was a slave's, the other a master's.

"I think you've earned the right to wear them both," he said.

"How did you know, sir?" I asked many months later.

"Instinct," he said. "I can tell when a man's ass is hungry. Or when he needs the pain he gives others. There are lots of men like that, too many, and most not worth their salt. But I knew you'd be worth it. I could tell by the way you handled Gene."

"Thank you, sir."

"I also knew that you needed what I could give you."

"Thank you, sir."

I let a moment pass, then spoke again.

"Sir?"

"Slave?"

"Who gives you what you give me when you need it?"

He was silent a while and I was afraid that I'd made him angry. Then he threw back his head and laughed his wicked laugh.

"Who, indeed!" He laughed harder than before. I grew afraid.

"The circle is complete," he finally said when he'd regained himself. "My master..." He smiled broadly as he shared his secret, pausing for effect. "My master is Gene."

I thought he was kidding me at first, then knew he wasn't. It was too perfect, the cosmic joke. I was my slave's slave's slave, my master's master's master. Betrayed by both, I felt I'd been honored and degraded in one decisive, impossible act of their combined wills. I was trapped, caught in a cyclone, not knowing where – or even if – I'd ever land.

Jack just laughed the louder.

THE CENTER OF THE MAZE

To burn with desire and keep quiet about it is the greatest punishment we can bring on ourselves.

- Frederico Garcia Lorca

Part One: Beginnings

Gene was in his last year of college and still naive in some ways. He was clean shaven, almost handsome. Some men thought he was pretty, but he wasn't, just good looking in a fair haired, boyish sort of way.

Aaron was more than handsome. Dark haired, bearded, with powerful shoulders and a lean torso, and hairy all over. He was wearing worn jeans, black boots and no shirt when Gene saw him at Mona's Gorilla Lounge.

"A regular Neanderthal," a friend whispered in Gene's ear. Gene pushed his friend aside and approached Aaron who had matched his stare from the beginning.

"Wanna dance?" asked Gene.

"I'd rather make you dance."

"Pardon?"

"Let's go," said Aaron grabbing a leather jacket from a bar stool and walking out without a second glance.

Gene followed.

When he got outside, Aaron was already starting the bike. It had gotten chilly, and Gene needed the jacket he'd left in his car.

"Get on."

Gene obeyed wordlessly. The bike started and Gene clung to Aaron's body for warmth.

They headed not into town as Gene expected, but away from it and up into the Santa Cruz mountains. The air grew warmer as they drove away from the ocean and Gene stopped shivering. They stopped at a house secluded by redwoods.

"The place belongs to a friend. I live in the City."

"Oh."

"What's your name, boy?"

Gene wasn't sure he liked being called 'boy.'

"Gene. What's yours?"

"You can call me 'sir.'"

Gene laughed nervously.

Aaron opened the door and with a firm hand on Gene's butt, led him into the house.

When he was bent over Aaron's lap and spanked with gloved hand, Gene couldn't resist. His heart raced and his cock hardened. He resisted the impulse to think about where he was or what was happening. If he thought about it, he knew, he would panic. Instead of thinking, he closed his eyes, breathed deep, and whispered, "Thank you."

Aaron gave orders and Gene obeyed. Aaron bound Gene and beat him, tormented him in ways Gene had never imagined. In a few hours, overwhelmed with sensation, Gene was no longer able to respond to Aaron's ministrations. His body numb, his mind foggy, he felt only gratitude for what had been given him. "Thank you, sir," he moaned again and again. "Thank you, thank you..."

So Aaron fucked him.

Gene was jolted, if not back into reality, then at least from where he'd been. He threw his ass upward to meet Aaron's cock as it pushed its way into his body. Aaron slammed himself against Gene's ass, and a contest of wills began. Each man sought to force the other to shoot first. To the winner went the power.

Aaron won.

Gene pushed his ass against Aaron's cock as it sawed him in two. He screamed like a man dying. His hole clenched around Aaron as Gene's own cock bounced into the air and shot, each spurt arching through the air like a rocket. He screamed again as Aaron's final, insistent thrusts pounded the tender prostate. Then Aaron screamed, his body and face tightened into a single knot of pain. Gene felt Aaron's cock pulse inside him, felt the force of Aaron's orgasm as it splashed against the walls of his guts.

It was good that Aaron had won the contest. If not, Aaron would not have consented to see Gene again. And Gene would have felt that he held Aaron in his hand and become the pushy bottom he was already hinting of becoming before he'd suddenly found himself mastered.

Every day for the next two weeks Gene went to the cabin in the redwoods. He passed from pleasure/pain to pain/pleasure in a single night. Now he had only to explore the varieties of pain that he might find pleasure in.

A week later Gene was led, naked except for boots and wrist restraints, into the forest. Aaron told him to stand, feet wide apart, in a clearing between two trees. Each ankle was secured to the nearest trunk. Then his wrists were secured so that he was made to stand spread eagle in empty space. Aaron attached clamps to Gene's nipples, kissed him gently in the space between his shoulders and walked away. Gene heard the crunch of Aaron's footsteps on the forest floor, disappearing.

Gene felt excited at first. Then he felt nervous, abandoned. Finally he was terrified at being left so alone and so vulnerable for so long. He pulled at his restraints. His breathing was hard and heavy. He hyperventilated and slumped forward against his restraints, blacking out momentarily.

As he came to, Gene was aware of the tit clamps again. His cock was hard. He stood up straight, flexing as much of his body as he could. He found that if he flexed his shoulder and chest muscles, the chain attaching the tit clamps danced against his skin, tightening the clamps. He threw back his head and called out like a man having a vision. He flexed his whole body against the shackles, fucking the air with his hard dick.

He came.

His cum shot across the forest floor for several feet. His face twisted into a snarl that forced his eyes shut with spurt of his juices. He screamed ecstasy to the canopy of trees on the last shot of spunk. He felt his soul had been pulled through his cock, that he was left with only his depleted body, an empty shell.

He was light headed, bordering on euphoric, for some time. Then he felt something spreading in waves over his back and buttocks: Something like water only firmer, like fire only softer. He recognized the feel of the whip's sting-like a caress.

He moaned softly to himself. "Oh, yes," he murmured. "Yes, yes. Thank you..."

The whip's strength increased, forcing small, sharp cries from Gene. He closed his eyes and was at one with the rhythm of the whip, even at peace with it. He felt himself fall, felt the wind about him and heard the steady beat of the whip as it cracked against his skin.

His feet were no longer on solid ground and he wondered where he was, surrounded by darkness. He looked ahead of him with eyes closed and saw that he was in a maze, saw that he needed to turn one way or the other. He followed his intuition and turned left, then right, then left again.

The whip snapped along his back with greater urgency.

Gene increased his speed as made his way through the maze, turning one way then the other. Gene screamed, ran, turned a final time to what he was sure was the center of the maze –

Aaron was holding him in his great hairy arms, kissing him, spanking him, caressing him. He heard Aaron speak soothingly to him, speak with pride, assurance and (Gene hoped) love. Gene felt himself being released from his bonds, felt his stiff limbs being massaged, felt himself being carried off over Aaron's broad, muscular shoulder.

Gene felt uncertain, felt that something was still expected of him. He was also groggy and wanted to sleep for a very long time.

Aaron laid him down somewhere soft, lifted one leg over each shoulder, and fucked Gene's ass long and hard. Gene felt himself come around now, being fucked giving him the needed focus. He felt the huge cock rearrange his guts, push him inside out. He yelled out his joy again as the dickhead swelled and filled his hole with hot, sticky cream. Then he shot all over himself, like he had among the trees, without touching himself.

Aaron kissed him again. Gene felt the man's beard against his face, felt the man's sweat pour down on him. Gene raised his face to lick the sweat off of Aaron's body.

"You made it."

"I'm sorry?"

"You got there, to the other side of pain."

"I guess."

Gene tried to get out of bed and fell back on the mattress, unable to move.

"Take it easy," said Aaron handing Gene a mug of something hot. Gene accepted it with both hands.

"Thanks. Do I look as bad as I feel?"

Aaron caressed his cheek.

"You look fine. Your backside is a mess, is all. We drew blood."

"Oh."

"You'll feel better once you start moving around, but you'll be sore for a while. And you'll remember it for more than a few days."

"Thank you. Sir."

Aaron kissed Gene softly on the lips.

"But I feel like I missed something. Like I didn't get there at all."

Aaron nodded the negative.

"You went as far as you can go and still come back."

Gene shook his head, not quite understanding.

Aaron's stay in the house was over.

This did not surprise Gene. He had already reconciled himself to this eventuality. What he was uncertain of was his status in Aaron's life. Would Aaron allow Gene to follow him later?

"May I come and be your slave in the City?" asked Gene.

"Not right away. This is still new to you. You need to learn more about yourself first. In five years, if you still want to be my slave, I'll be your master."

Gene was still too young to see five years as anything less than an eternity. Aaron might as well have said five-thousand years.

"Why so long?"

"Then you'll be as old as I am now. It seems a good age to me."

"But what if you find another slave before then?"

"What if you find another master?"

There was a pause. Gene turned and looked at the welts and reddened flesh still healing across his back. He felt a rush pride in the marks, then a kind of disappointment, as if even they hadn't been enough to secure Aaron as his master.

"I make no promises," Gene finally said. "But if I decide to be another man's slave, I'll let you know."

Aaron nodded.

"But how will I find you?"

"It won't be so hard. Now why don't you be a good boy and bend over so I can fuck you until you bleed, one last time?"

Gene was glad to obey.

When Aaron left, Gene was several days into a beard. He decided to let it grow. It was his first beard. He saw another self emerge as the beard took shape.

Part Two: Finding the Way

When Gene arrived in San Francisco he learned that he had the kind of look that was currently popular. With his new beard, he was suddenly handsome, even hot.

Gene came into a modest trust fund. He wasn't rich, but neither did have to work very hard to live well. He took odd jobs that he enjoyed, jobs that were short term but interesting. His financial freedom allowed him to spend his nights exploring the maze of streets South of Market. Months could pass without Gene seeing a morning sky.

Sometimes he traveled.

Sometimes he saw Aaron.

The first few months in the City he lived in the Castro. Being naive, Gene assumed any man in leather would be willing and able to give him what Aaron had. After several disappointments (the last of which he told off saying, "You don't have the *right* to wear leather!") Gene decided that he belonged on Folsom Street.

He found a small flat on Raush Street. It had been empty for months and was cluttered with the remnants of the last tenant. Cleaning out the attic and closets of his new home he found odds and ends of black leather: belts, boots, straps, unmatched gloves, and a well worn motorcycle jacket.

A guy named Carl used to live there," said Jim, Gene's new upstairs neighbor. "He spent less and less time at home, then he disappeared without a word to anyone."

"What do you think happened?"

"There were some rumors. But there always are, so why listen?"

Gene nodded, not quite agreeing.

"Does the jacket fit you?"

"No. It's too big."

"Then sell it."

"I think I'll keep it," said Gene. "He might come back."

Gene made friends in his new neighborhood. First he met Jim, who lived in the flat upstairs from him. Through Jim he met Alan, whose master was a cop. The youngest member of the group was Will, whom Gene met walking alone on Folsom Street after three o'clock one morning. They were a society of friends, tight knit and watchful of each other. They met at the Eagle before the eleven o'clock crush, talked about men they met, their jobs and room mates. Gene said little, confiding only in Jim, his closest friend and occasional fuck buddy.

Saying little, Gene was a good listener and heard details of each man's life that no one else heard. He heard tales others would disbelieve and accepted them without judgment.

"It wasn't an accident," said Jim one rainy afternoon in Gene's apartment. "It happened because you wanted it to happen. Isn't that what you'd tell me?"

Gene handed Jim a mug of coffee. A neighbor's cat had come in from the rain and lay sleeping on the radiator. Jim eyed the cat wearily.

Gene had told Jim about Aaron and the maze. Now he felt relieved, tired, like a Catholic after confession.

"I wondered what your story was," added Jim. "I was sure you had one."

Gene smiled, sipped his coffee.

"I saw him last night on Dore Alley."

"Did he see you?"

"Yeah. He nodded and I went over to say hello. Instead I just licked his leather jacket."

"What happened?" Jim was excited by the story.

"He held me for a while, kissed me, and sent me on my way."

"Did he say anything?"

"Not with words."

Jim made a noise somewhere between a snort and a sigh that said he wasn't satisfied with the answer.

"Well, what did he say *without* words?"

"That he loved me."

They sat for a while without speaking.

"How much longer?"

"It's only been a year. Four more."

Jim sighed again.

"I wouldn't do it," he said. "Life's too short to wait for love. Or for a master, for that matter. Masters are men like us, Gene. And men like us change."

Gene nodded, but not in agreement.

"This man waits, but not alone. Are you up for the slot tonight, Jimbo? I already reserved a room for us."

Alan's master kicked Alan out.

Alan spent hours on the phone with Gene while he hid himself away in a new apartment. After half a year, Alan reappeared on Folsom Street for a few months. He was aloof, though, almost unfriendly towards Gene and the others, especially to Will who taken Alan's place as Officer Jackson's slave. Strangely, it was Will who kept insisting he'd seen Alan around the neighborhood at night when no on else had.

Then Alan disappeared altogether, leaving his apartment and belongings unclaimed. There were rumors, of course, but no facts.

Jim dismissed it all. Gene felt a chill run through him whenever he thought about it.

A year later Gene went alone to the Caldron. He was leaning against a wall, naked except for chaps and boots, watching two men fuck with a shared fury, slamming against each other, shooting off sparks of dissipating rage.

"Fuck you! Fuck you! Fuck you!" bellowed the top with each slam into his partner's butt.

"Motherfucker!" screamed the bottom. "Motherfucking bastard!"

Gene watched the scene, his face expressionless while his heart raced with excitement. His cock got larger, filled with blood, but he didn't touch himself, not wanting to cum yet.

He felt a hand on his cock and turned to see who it was. If he was hot, then Gene might let him continue. Gene liked what he saw: a curly haired man-boy whose chin just reached Gene's shoulder.

The man-boy was dark, clean shaven but with the shadow of stubble apparent even in the dim light of the Caldron. His chest and torso were covered with soft, curly hair that grew like some furry vegetation out of his undone jeans. His bright blue eyes asked the question, "May I?", even as his full lips reached up towards Gene's mouth for an answer.

"I'm going to fuck that pretty mouth," thought Gene as their lips met. The next instant Gene's arms were around the man-boy, holding him close to Gene's body, holding him still as Gene's tongue fucked the man-boy's mouth. The man-boy returned Gene's embrace, succumbed to the assault without resistance, responded in kind.

The kiss lasted forever.

Gene closed his eyes. He was back in the maze.

The man-boy's mouth broke from Gene's, attached itself to Gene's armpit. Keeping his eyes closed, Gene wrapped an arm around the man-boy's head as the sweat pouring from his body was eagerly lapped up from the twin hairy pools. After a time there, the man-boy's attention wandered to Gene's nipples which were chewed and sucked.

Gene made soft low moans that echoed into the maze. Keeping his eyes shut, Gene not so much saw, but sensed the light not far from where he was. He moved toward it.

He was kissing the man-boy again, penetrating the strange, soft throat with his tongue.

Further, Gene thought, further. I can get there in time.

The man-boy licked the sweat from Gene's face and beard. Gene pushed him down to his knees where Gene's hard cock found the wet warmth of the stranger's mouth. Gene lost himself in the maze of delight as the man-boy's throat pulled and sucked at the stiff rod sliding between two perfect lips.

141

Gene no longer ran through the maze. He flew. His urgency increased with the pace of their sex.

Gene's crotch slammed against the man-boy's face as he fucked "that pretty mouth." He felt two hands pull on his tits, increasing the urgency he felt, the urge to shoot, the urge to reach the center of the maze.

Gene's mouth hung open, panting like an excited animal. A third mouth joined his in a long, deliberate kiss.

Gene was almost there. He could see the light.

With the kiss, Gene cried out, pulled the man-boy's head tightly to his groin and shot his load down the man-boy's gagging throat.

He came too soon. He was back at the Caldron. A crowd had gathered around him.

"Shit," said one man.

"Hot fucker," said another.

"I wanna fuck that pretty face next," said a third.

Gene broke away from the kiss that held him as he came. He opened his eyes and saw that he'd been kissing Jim.

"All right!" said Jim.

The man-boy continued sucking on Gene's softening dick, licking up the last few drops oozing from his piss slit. Gene slowly pulled out of the stranger's mouth and lifted the man boy to his feet. They embraced, kissed deeply, if tenderly this time.

"He came on your leathers," said Jim.

"He can lick it up later."

Gene and the man-boy kissed a long, deep kiss again. This time Gene tasted the traces of his own salty cum.

"What's your name, cocksucker?"

"Erin, sir."

Gene shook his head, not quite believing his ears.

"Hey, buddy, let me have a taste," said Jim waving his hard-on in a gloved hand.

Gene nodded vaguely at Erin who dropped to his knees and sucked Jim dry while he and Gene kissed.

"Fucking fantastic," said Jim a few minutes later as he tucked his dick back into his jeans. "Say, pal, let me have a crack at his other hole some time – *after* you've had it."

Jim kissed Gene while giving him a smack on the butt.

"I'll call you tomorrow."

Gene nodded, his attention now fully focused on the precious man-boy standing before him, looking into his face expectantly.

"Sir?"

Gene brought Erin home that night, tied him to the bed and whipped him soundly with the length of an English riding crop. The whipping was methodical, lacking sensuality, warmth or passion. He whipped Erin until he drew blood.

When Gene stood back to admire what he'd done to Erin's smooth flesh, he noticed that Erin was whimpering from the pain, wanting/needing comfort. Gene ignored him. Instead, Gene poured hot wax on the worst lacerations, stuffing Erin's mouth with a dirty sock to keep him from screaming. Satisfied with his handiwork, Gene fucked/raped Erin's ass without bothering to lubricate cock or hole. Erin's muffled screams only excited him more.

Gene's orgasm was fierce, shaking his entire body and covering them both with sweat. He lay on top of Erin for more than an hour afterwards, thinking, wondering at how, after all this, he felt so dissatisfied. Finally, he got up and untied the shaking, frightened Erin, held him close and kissed him tenderly as he stroked the man-boy's cock to an impressive climax.

"You hurt me."

"You wanted me to hurt you."

"Yes, but..."

"But, what?"

"Not like that."

"Like what?"

"So cruel."

"Love is cruel. And I love you very much."

They became lovers, almost to the exclusion of all other partners or friends. Erin moved in, went to work everyday, and handed his paycheck to Gene every other Friday. Gene locked a chain dog collar on Erin's neck and refused to remove it, even when Erin went to work.

Only Jim ever visited the flat upstairs. Every few days he came by to fuck Erin, or lay back and watch himself be serviced by a pair of perfect lips.

Erin and Gene lived for each other, for the power of their kisses, for the physical torment and cruel sex that Gene insisted they continue. He tried to explain to Erin about the maze, about finding its center. Erin understood only the concept. He didn't understand how his bruised and punished body aided Gene in his quest, or even why it was so important.

In the end, Gene went to far, sending Erin over the edge into unconsciousness. Badly frightened, Erin moved out the next day without a word.

Gene found Erin a week later.

"Don't touch me!"

"I won't. I just came to say I'm sorry. Here's the money from your pay checks. I don't need it and you do. I should never have done what I did. I never found the maze again, not since that first time in the Caldron. I thought I would because I loved you so much."

Erin took the money without looking at it.

"I loved you, too."

Gene handed Erin the key to the collar still secured around his neck.

"You left," said Gene. "It's up to you to release yourself."

Part Three: Found / A Conclusion

"Kink chic is a thing of the past," Jim said. "The clones have hung their leathers out at garage sales and retreated back to their ghetto."

"And left us to ourselves," added Gene.

It was late on a rainy Sunday afternoon. Out of boredom, they'd decided to get drunk. Jim barely finished two beers, and Gene had drunk even less. This didn't matter though, since the fun was in the intention to get drunk rather than actually getting there.

Jim was the only one left, along with Gene, from their original quartet of friends. Their friendship increased in intensity over the years, despite quarrels and jealousies.

Erin stayed with Jim for a while, but Jim never offered to share him with Gene as they normally shared their lovers, slaves and (occasionally) masters. Gene for his part was always solicitous of Erin, but never suggested they have sex again.

"Things have changed so much," Jim went on, waxing on as he did when he was with Gene. "Half the guys have shaved off their beards."

"What's become of the world?" laughed Gene. "Where are the standards of yesterday?"

They laughed together, even in their shared sadness. Their world had changed radically overnight, and they mourned for it as much older men mourn for their youth. Bars and clubs closed. Folsom's character changed, at least superficially: Straight clubs opened, along with trendy restaurants, condominiums and mainstream businesses. That they would eventually be forced out of their homes, their community fragmented by urban renewal, was inevitable.

"Five years ago the only people who'd look out of place at Hamburger Mary's were the breeders slumming from the fern bars on Union Street," Jim complained. "Now it's full of them. Fucking yups."

Gene nodded his agreement, feeling the same anger as his friend.

Occasionally, late at night when the one or two surviving leather bars had closed, Gene would walk along the streets and alleys he knew so well, and still feel something like he used to feel: A dark, warm intimacy that was at once cold and comforting, like the fog. But it was also like seeing an old friend again, and Gene would open his arms to embrace it, only to find the moment, and the feeling, gone.

There was less action now, but with a few adaptations, Gene and Jim (who professed a secret and long standing condom fetish) continued their lives as they had before.

"Just as well we're losing Folsom, though," Jim said with some finality. "The whole neighborhood is built on swamp, you know. They didn't fill it in right and the buildings are sinking. Like ours. Ever notice how low the first basement step is? Hell, let the breeders have it!"

"The question is, Jimbo, whether or not we're going to go down with it."

This was supposed to have been a joke to cheer Jim up. It had the opposite effect.

"Hell," said Jim. "Let's sink with it."

"Sure," said Gene. "We'll be another lost civilization."

Gene bottomed less and less. He was so experienced in the art of being a slave that he found few men worthy of the gift of his submission. Filling the void, he spent more and more of his time as a top. He took special care in molding new slaves and novices, taking them step by step to the entrance of the maze. Those who were unsure of themselves became frightened and ran. Those who had at last found their life's destiny entered the maze without hesitation. These men Gene came to cherish, even love, as men cherish their children.

He realized the obvious about the maze: It was entered by letting go. He had tried to force the experience before and so only experienced it when he was caught off guard. Now he stayed in the maze for longer periods of time, hoping that by delaying the final twist of the journey, he'd at last see the center.

Without mentioning it, he brought other men to the maze through pain and pleasure, escorting them in, then letting them run wild in its shadows. But as he showed men this new and, to Gene, sacred place, he also observed that he alone wanted to see the center.

"See the center?" he'd ask. "Don't you want to see the center of the maze?"

See the center?" men would respond. "There's no light in the maze to see it. Only darkness. It's as if the shadows have shadows."

"The dark doesn't scare you?"

"No. It feels safe, familiar – like Folsom Street after the bars close, but long before dawn."

Gene thought he understood.

Jim suggested they go to the leather dance after the Folsom Street Fair.

"When was the last time you danced in your leathers?" asked Jim.

"I don't remember the date, but I know I was with you. It was the Black Party, I think. Sylvester sang. We separated after two o'clock and you disappeared for a few weeks."

Jim smiled, remembering.

"It will be fun," said Gene.

"Maybe it will be like the old days..."

"Right, Jimbo. We'll do drugs, snort poppers and fuck strangers."

"That's not what I meant, Gene. I was talking about the music."

"Sure, Jimbo. Maybe they'll play the old stuff."

Gene went to the dance wearing a pair of leather shorts he'd bought in Amsterdam, the boots he'd gotten in London on the same trip, and fingerless gloves. Jim wore chaps with a leather jock and uniform boots. Both were shirtless, wearing only arm bands over both biceps.

Jim had a new tattoo – an eagle landing over his left pec, the talons closing on Jim's pierced nipple – that he'd been showing off all day at the Street Fair. Gene envied Jim's courage in decorating his body as he chose. Instead, Gene waited for Aaron to decide how and when his own body would be adorned.

They stayed together for a time, dancing, talking, watching sweaty men dance in clusters or pairs. Jim saw Erin stumbling drunk across the dance floor. A hot man wasted, Jim thought, but said nothing to Gene.

They stood together, but not together, each waiting for either the other's signal to part company or the distraction of sex.

A young man, neatly muscled and smooth skinned, wearing only dungarees and sneakers paused to glance at Jim. Jim looked back and decided the man was too young, hardly more than a boy and easily dismissed despite a certain shaggy-haired charm. But then the boy reached out to caress Jim's new tattoo with something like reverence. Jim grabbed the boy's hand, pulled him close, hoping the suddenness of his action would scare the boy off. Instead, the boy licked the sweat from Jim's body, starting with the tattoo, finding his way to Jim's leather jock, and finally his boots. He might have been too young to normally appeal to Jim, too smooth and precious, but the kid had style. Jim rearranged his crotch beneath the leather to keep his hard cock safe within its confines until he got the kid home.

Jim looked around and saw that Gene had already disappeared.

Gene had seen Aaron standing in a shadowed corner on the edge of the dance floor just as the boy had approached Jim. Now Gene was standing before the man, offering himself. He knelt, crawled on his stomach and kissed Aaron's boots.

Men on the dance floor stopped to watch.

Gene was licking Aaron's boots now, making his way up to his master's knees.

"You're mine," Aaron half-shouted above the music.

"Yes, master," Gene yelled in response. "Always."

"You shit head," Jim said a few days latter over the phone. "You and your daddy upstaged me and the boy."

"And I wasn't even trying."

"Bastard."

"So who's the kid?"

"Name's Tim. From the River, he says. Before that from some hell hole near Tahoe. Used to hustle. Think I should put him on the streets for me?"

"Is that all he's good for? Can't he cook?"

"Don't know. Makes a handy foot stool, though. In fact, that's what he's doing now."

"Talk about bastards."

"I try. So how about you? You're Aaron's boy, right? You moving in with him?"

"Soon. Right now I'm putting things in order. Then we're going to Europe. He says he wants to lead me on a leash down Warmoesstraat."

"Sounds romantic."

"Won't be the first time."

"Slut."

"I try, Jimbo, I try."

Being a slave, or at least Aaron's slave, was harder than Gene had anticipated. Not because Gene failed or refused to be submissive, but because they were so obviously equals – intellectually, spiritually, economically. While Aaron was a professional who could easily have supported them both, for instance, Gene neither desired nor needed that support and continued to work whenever he felt the urge.

Since it was only in physical size and strength that Aaron was clearly Gene's superior, Gene's status as slave was established and maintained by symbols that held more power for both master and slave than chains and shackles. Gene always called Aaron "sir" or "master," even in public, and refrained from sitting on the furniture without permission when Aaron was at home. Gene's right ear lobe and both nipples were pierced in a public ritual at the Catacombs. Aaron locked a collar around Gene's neck and stored the key in a safe deposit box. More important to both of them, though, Aaron made certain that healing somewhere on Gene's body was a welt or bruise inflicted by Aaron's own hand to remind Gene of his status.

Gene had kept a journal since his first encounter with Aaron. Now he spent hours reading and re-reading it, searching for clues to the maze. He spent even more time writing in his journal, recalling again and again the events that led him to where he was, and speculated on what he would find when, and if, he found the center of the maze. At times, he feared it.

Aaron wanted to know more about the maze, listened carefully to the words Gene used to describe the experience, and soon he was in the maze with Gene, and like Gene, searching for it's center.

Their intimacy increased. Gene saw his friends only while Aaron worked or was out of town. Each night they were together they made the journey: Gene was bound, gagged, chained, beaten, and tortured until his balls exploded cum across the room, and each time they both felt closer to the center.

Before leaving for Europe, Aaron was away on business and Gene spent an evening with Jim and Jim's new boy. Keeping his slave collar on, as he did at all times, Gene fucked Timmy-boy (as Jim called him) repeatedly.

"You're less than a slave," Gene told him. "You're being fucked by another slave."

Jim laughed.

"Tell him, Gene, buddy! Tell the dog what he is!"

When Gene felt himself ready to cum up Tim's butthole, he slapped the boy's ass cheeks as hard as he could. The hole tightened around his shooting cock. Gene hollered his victory as he emptied his balls into the rubber.

When he pulled out a moment later, Gene tied the used condom into a knot and tossed it to Tim.

"Something to remember me by."

When they were done using him, Timmy-boy was sent to another room while his master and Gene talked, as they always did, about everything and nothing. Mostly they laughed.

"I notice you let the cats get on the furniture but not the boy," observed Gene.

"Cat's can't be owned and ordered about. Only dogs. Dogs are born to be ruled, and since Tim's a dog, he does what he's told. That much he understands."

They laughed long and hard.

"I'll miss you, Gene. How long will you be gone?"

"A couple months. I'll write. I'll bring you something back from Europe. They've got some nasty leathers in Amsterdam that you'll love."

Jim sighed.

"I'll miss you, babe," he said. "Be careful for me, okay? Timmy-boy and I will be here when you get back."

Gene had been to Amsterdam before and thought that he knew it well – its leather bars, canals, boy brothels, cafes, back rooms, museums and sex shops. But Aaron had other connections, knew where the private black rooms were and how to access them.

Gene was impressed. Impressed to be shackled by iron chains to an ancient stone wall. Impressed to be blind-folded and left to the care of strangers, strangers who only spoke to each in Nederland. Impressed to have spent a night in continual sexual subservience to a pack of men who barked orders and laughed at his humiliation. A sack of used condoms was given to him in the morning, symbolic reminders of his status as fuck hole. After that he'd been brought to another room and allowed to sleep on a bare cot for what seemed like too short a time.

Gene hadn't seen Aaron since the night before. He imagined his master fucking and whipping some Dutch boy, slamming the too pale skin with all his dark fury. Gene's cock hardened thinking about such a scene, and only hoped Aaron had saved some of that delicious rage for him.

A fire burned near by in the narrow room and Gene felt its warmth flickering on his bare skin. He put his face to the stone wall and felt its coolness, smelled the city's pervading dampness. He pulled on the chains that held him. Relieved at the hopelessness of escape, his cock stayed hard.

> He turned and saw that he was in the maze, a place where four paths met. He turned slowly in a circle and chose a path: There, that one. Where the darkness was deepest, where the shadows had shadows.

Gene felt the feathery touch of a gloved hand softly stroke the smoothness of his taut skin. He knew at once it was Aaron's touch.

"I bought a new whip."

"Thank you, sir."

The whipping began.

He turned and saw Aaron next to him. Together they found their way through the blackness, seeing walls, doors and windows of the maze in their minds.

Gene felt flowers of fire blossoming over his back, shoulders and buttocks – felt them turn to ice, then back to fire, over and over again. The flowers never stopped blooming.

He heard himself cry out.

They held back this time, refusing to hurry. Almost touching, but never quite.

Aaron's cock, engorged and fat with blood and cum, swung free and ready.

Aaron felt the sweat drip from his body. He was exhausted, but afraid to pause. If he did, they might lose their way. He concentrated on Gene's body as it writhed in its steel shackles. He watched, heard Gene's moans, then his screams.

Someone said something to Aaron. The voice was concerned. Aaron heard the question and raised the whip to strike Gene's battered body again as his only response.

Gene's cock was hard. He felt it fuck the air as they flew through space, felt the universe suck it with a warm, wet throat. "Yes," he said. "Show it to us and we'll give to you. But show us the center first." He followed his cock as it soared across the sky, turned and saw Aaron beside him, flying on the power of his own enormous member, dripping sweetness...

Aaron's hand never stopped beating Gene's body with methodical calm. His face was blank, broken only by a small smile when he whipped Gene's hard dick.

They were still together, now, almost but not quite. Almost there but not quite.

The last moment before orgasm is anguish. It lasts forever.

They were there, even in the darkness. They touched, joined. Both men screamed, feeling cum gush from their dicks, cum springing not just from their balls, but from their guts as well, from the center of the solar plexus.

They were together, joined for an eternity. They saw the center at last. Together.

The light was blinding.

First they heard the sound of their own breathing. Then each was able to separate the sound of his own breathing from the other's. Then they heard concerned voices speaking loudly, words Gene didn't understand.

Gene felt many hands lift him, carry him away, bathe him, caress him, put him to bed.

After he'd slept for most of a day, Gene lifted his head from the pillow just long enough to see Aaron near by, staring into space, saying nothing. Curling himself into a ball, as an animal does to keep warm, Gene fell back to sleep until the next morning.

Gene came home alone.

Aaron went south to Crete.

"Amsterdam is best for leather clothes and toys. And SM porno. But London is best for boots and whips."

"Is that where you got that one?" asked Jim, pointing to a whip hung over the mantel like an icon.

"I think that's where Aaron got it," said Gene. "I wasn't with him at the time. I was only there for its inauguration."

There was a comfortable pause as Jim admired himself again in the leather uniform shirt Gene had brought him from Amsterdam.

"Gene, where's Aaron?"

"He's staying in Europe for a while."

"You're not wearing your collar anymore."

"No, I'm not. What about Timmy-boy?"

"Gone. Disappeared one day."

They returned to their comfortable silence.

THE OTHER SIDE

And what should I do Illyria?
My brother, he is in Elysium.

-William Shakespeare

Those to whom
The night of earth gives benediction
Should not be mourned. Retribution comes.

-Sophocles

Gene's death was neither surprising nor expected. He had lived so close to the edge for so long that sudden death, even from "natural causes", seemed only appropriate. But Jim and Gene had been best friends, occasional fuck buddies and neighbors for most of their adult lives, and Jim was unprepared for this sudden desertion. The money Gene left to him (all he had had, which, while not a fortune was substantial enough) did nothing to ease Jim's pain.

Like most of his friends, Jim survived, but remained unaccustomed to the constant presence of death. Gene's death was the final blow that sent him into a deep depression. For the better part of a year he avoided the people, parties and bars that reminded him of Gene. He went to work, came home, and answered the phone so rarely that he wondered why he bothered paying the phone bill at all. His single comfort was the container holding Gene's ashes. Sitting prominently on the mantel of his narrow front room, they let Jim feel that he was still close to Gene, still near the man he'd loved more than any lover.

After their birthdays (a week apart) came and went uncelebrated in October, followed by the holidays that passed unobserved, Gene woke one morning to discover the winter rains were gone and that he was still alive. Suddenly aware that the anniversary of Gene's death had come and gone and that he'd survived without the expected devastation, he knew that a life without Gene was possible. He went back to the gym, cleaned out the boxes of Gene's belongings cluttering his apartment, and bought himself a first class ticket to Amsterdam with some of the money Gene had left him. He found a map of Amsterdam among Gene's affects and located the bridge crossing the Keizersgracht, where, according to Gene's wishes, he would drop Gene's ashes.

Standing on the bridge a few weeks later, Jim felt the old sadness wash over him, felt the finality of letting go of his best friend. But the urn felt heavy in his hands now, and he let it slip though his fingers as he knew he must, watching it fall soundlessly into the murky water below.

He waited a few minutes before walking away, looking back only once at the silent, dark water.

Feeling strangely satisfied with himself for fulfilling this last obligation to his friend, and since it was already past midnight, Jim headed towards the leather bars on Warmoesstraat. Gene had praised Amsterdam's men and leather bars for as long as Jim could remember; he wished now that he and Gene had gotten around to making the trip together like they'd planned. He walked into the Argos and asked for a beer. Toasting the empty air with the bottle, he said half aloud, "Gene, buddy, this is for you."

Waking up the next morning was like emerging from darkness, struggling for the light like a drowning man struggles for air. With effort he opened his eyes to find he was in a strange bed in a strange room. A familiar looking man sat naked at a table drinking coffee and reading a newspaper. The man looked up, saw Jim was awake and smiled.

"Good morning."

The voice, the gentle accent, was enough to refresh Jim's memory. He remembered meeting him the night before at the Argos, remembered kissing him and then being forced to his knees to suck the Dutchman's fat cock. After that, there was only a blur.

"Morning, Pieter."

"Coffee?"

"Please."

He was stiff all over, his butt soar and bruised. Pieter had obviously beaten his ass, but Jim remembered only a few odd images of the night before: Pieter in leather, the canal in the moonlight, the sensation of being spanked and fucked. Oddly, though, it was as if these images had been observed from the outside, as if he'd been watching a film of the night before even as he experienced it.

"Are you all right?"

"I think so. Did we get stoned last night?"

"You did no shit while you were with me. Maybe before?"

"No, no. All I had was that one beer. But it's been so long since I drank at all, maybe..."

"Are you worried about something? I did use a rubber, Jim."

"I remember that much," Jim lied.

He stretched as he got out of bed, discovering his body no worse off than it had been a thousand times before after such nights, nights when he did remember what had happened. He came to the table and helped himself to a *broodje*. "Thank you, Pieter."

"*Alstublieft*. Tell me, Jim, how long are you here?"

"A couple weeks, I think. There's a lot I want to see and do. Like get some new leathers."

"I will go with you to Rob's if you like."

"Yes, that would be nice."

"Jim? What do your friends call you? Jimmy?"

Jim swallowed his coffee before answering.

"My best friend used to call me Jimbo."

"Jimbo?" laughed Pieter. "Yes, I like Jimbo."

Returning with a second suitcase filled with new leathers and toys, Jim headed home. As much as he'd enjoyed Europe, he wanted to see his friends again, to return to his old life. Exhausted from his last night in Amsterdam, spent servicing Pieter's cock, balls and boots, he quickly fell asleep on the plane, muttering to himself as the plane ascended:

"Don't worry, Gene. I'll be back to visit. Soon. I love you, buddy, better than anyone. And I always will."

He fell asleep dreaming of the slow, dark currents covering Gene's grave.

The light seemed even further off than before, but he was heading towards it, fighting for it as he had the first time. Summoning all his strength, he opened his eyes and saw he was home, saw his cats watching him cautiously from the top of a bookcase. He smiled at the familiar surroundings, then realized the last thing he remembered was being on the plane. He got up and winced at the pain that shot through him. He looked at himself in the mirror and almost cried out loud at the number of welts that covered his body. He tried to remember something, anything, but recalled only a few jumbled images. As if remembering a dream, whatever he might recall was lost when he tried to put it in context. He wanted to talk to someone about this, but could think of no one but Gene. Gene would know, he thought, Gene would listen and not think I'm crazy.

He went into the kitchen to make coffee. Turning on the radio he discovered that he'd lost several days. He walked around the flat looking for clues and found his bags, still unpacked in the hallway by the stair. In the bathroom he found the shower curtain was damp. He could almost remember taking a shower, feeling the hot water flow over him. And as he remembered that, it seemed he could also recall getting fucked, feeling a familiar fat dick sliding in and out of him. He could even remember the hard, hairy body thrashing against his backside. But whose? He glanced into the toilet and saw a used condom floating in the water. At least he'd been safe.

He hoped he remembered enough to remember more. He disliked being confused, piecing together what had happened. If Gene were alive, Jim thought, he'd remember for me like he did when we were just a couple kids out of college, getting stoned and getting laid and only half-remembering what we'd done the next morning. This was a lot like the day after one of those parties. But unlike then, he wasn't so sure that he'd had such a good time.

The phone rang. It was Aaron, Gene's lover.

"How are you feeling after last night?"

"Okay," Jim answered automatically. "A little stiff."

"You really took it, you know. I see now why you and Gene were such good friends; you're as hot as he was. I had a real good time. Tell me when you're up for it again."

Jim stopped breathing. While he and Gene had shared their tricks and lovers, passing them back and forth as casually as they shared the contents of each other's refrigerators, Jim had never played with Aaron. Even when Gene wasn't seeing him, Jim knew that Aaron, the one great love in Gene's life, was off limits. Now he learned that he had betrayed Gene, but couldn't remember doing it. He felt sick to his stomach.

"Jim?"

"Yeah. Sure, Aaron. I'd like that. Anytime." he said automatically.

"Call me when you're ready to do it again."

"You bet."

He hung up the phone, crying aloud to the empty room, "Gene. I'm sorry!"

———✦———

Friends calmed Jim as best they could. "You're just stressed out, Jim," one said. "Don't let yourself get any crazier than you already are." But nothing changed. He continued to miss time. Friends remembered conversations Jim didn't remember having. After a while, Jim stopped saying anything about it, afraid people would think him insane. Gene was the only one, he was certain, who would have understood and had an explanation. The crazier things became, the more he thought of Gene and the dark waters entombing his friend's ashes.

He went to an S/M party a few months after he got back. It was the first time he'd been to a play party in over a year. Old friends, both his and Gene's, greeted him warmly, asked when he'd be available to play that evening. They admired his new leathers and wanted to know about Amsterdam and his adventures there. Wasn't Amsterdam as wonderful as Gene had said it was? Jim laughed to himself, remembering what Gene had enjoyed saying about the leather clad, tattooed and pierced women and men who were their friends: "Who ever thought jaded decadence would be so warm and supportive?"

Turning from a cluster of friends he was suddenly confronted with the angriest face he'd ever seen.

"You bastard," said the stranger. "You fucking bastard!"

Before anyone knew what was happening, the stranger's hands were locked around Jim's throat. A struggle followed and the stranger, someone new to the City, was pulled off of Jim. The dungeon monitor arrived and threw the newcomer out of the party without bothering to hear much of what he had to say. Jim, after all, was well known, and the stranger was just that - a stranger. It was impossible for anyone to believe what the stranger had said, that Jim had brutalized him, gagged and ignored him when he tried to signal for Jim to slow down or stop his beating. It was too incredible.

"The weirdest part of all," said the dungeon monitor after the stranger had been thrown out onto the street, "is that he said you're name was Gene. I told him he was crazy, Jim. I said Gene was dead and you'd been out of circulation."

Jim felt a cold shudder run through him. He didn't remember the man at all, but he remembered so little now a days. Hours of everyday were missing. How many mornings had he woken up certain that something had happened the night before but just as uncertain of what that something had been? He felt close to panic. Looking badly shaken as he did, Steve offered to take Jim home. Glad of the company, and afraid to be alone, Jim convinced his friend to not only spend the night, but to tie him up and fuck him as well. Comforted as he always was by bondage, Jim clung to Steve all night long.

Then Aaron called saying he'd found a message on his answering machine from someone claiming to be Gene.

"The weirdest part of it, Jim, was that he sounded like Gene. Or a lot like Gene did. It's hard to explain."

Jim's first reaction was jealousy, that Gene had called Aaron and not himself. Then a sudden, but now familiar, chill came over him, an inner certainty that frightened him. "Sometimes," Gene once told him, "the unreal is very real. It's only unreal because we're unused to it."

"What did he say?" asked Jim, interrupting his own train of thought.

"Just that he'd been having a great time and would see me around. Here, let me play it for you."

Jim listened, feeling at the same time very unsettled and strangely comforted at the sound of the familiar voice. Only it wasn't Gene's voice exactly. It was Gene's flat California accent, his intonation and inflection, but the voice itself was someone else's, however familiar.

"Weird, huh?"

"What should we do?"

"Do? See if he calls back."

"Gene!" Jim said aloud after he'd said good-bye to Aaron. "Gene! You're dead! Stay dead and get out of my life!"

For a while things seemed back to normal. Days and nights, each accounted for, passed into weeks. He woke many mornings with Aaron's cock up his ass, but never wondered how he'd gotten there or how the bruises covering his backside had been inflicted. He stopped feeling guilty about being Aaron's lover, deciding that Gene would have approved. He'd have said something like, "Keeping it all in the family, Jimbo!" Jim remembered Gene often, remembered him and smiled or wept, but always with love. One Sunday morning, as they were lazing in bed with coffee and the Sunday paper, Aaron suggested that they travel to Amsterdam together. Jim agreed at once, thinking of Pieter and the other men he'd met there.

"And I want to see where you left Gene's ashes," Aaron added. "It's near the Homomonument?"

"The bridge on Westermarkt overlooking it."

Aaron nodded, and smiling asked, "He didn't ask for the red light district?"

Jim laughed as Aaron moved towards him, held him down and kissed him.

"Did I say you could laugh, boy?" asked Aaron, reaching for Jim and tickling him.

"No, sir. I'm sorry, sir. Oh, god, stop! Please, Daddy. Oh, shit."

Aaron stopped tickling and kissed him instead. A moment later they were fucking.

Gene, thought of Jim as he fell into a post-coital slumber in Aaron's arms a half-hour later.

"Gene, buddy, we're coming to see you soon," he murmured to himself. He could feel the dark water of the canal cover him as he fell asleep.

Jim would remember only walking to the bridge overlooking the canal where he'd dropped the urn holding Gene's ashes. He stood with Aaron in silence a while, waiting for the moment to pass, for Aaron to lead him across the bridge and back to their hotel room. Letting Aaron have his private moment, Jim stared into the murky waters and whispered Gene's name into the damp breeze. After that he remembered nothing.

"Come one Aaron, let's fuck," said a familiar voice. Aaron knew it had to be Jim, but at the same time didn't think it was the quiet, thoughtful man he'd walked there with only a moment before. He turned and saw Jim smiling, but the smile was out of place, like a photograph with someone else's smile pasted on it.

"Jim?"

"Of course. Who else would it be?"

Then there was a laugh, but not Jim's laugh, a laugh as out of place as the smile had been.

"Sure, Gene, let's fuck."

"Yeah, Daddy. I need it bad."

"Dybbuk," whispered Aaron through closed teeth. "Dybbuk!"

Jim's face looked bewildered, puzzled.

"What?"

Aaron grabbed Jim's shoulders and shook him as hard as he dared.

"I know it's you Gene. I know it! What the hell are you doing in there? What have you done with Jim?"

"Jim's safe enough. He's just – somewhere else right now."

Aaron followed the gaze to the water beneath them.

"You've no right!"

"No? Then why does he keep cooperating? Why does he keep calling me?"

"Because he loves you, still misses you. But that doesn't give you the right –"

"Right? What right do I have to live at all, you mean? I don't like it there in the dark. I like the light. And Jim lets me."

Aaron held Jim/Gene close, as if he were about to kiss him. Their lips almost touching.

"I can make you leave, Gene. I can force you out, but it will hurt. And you'll never see the light again."

"And what if I go back on my own? More darkness? Besides I don't think you really know –"

Aaron whispered words in Jim/Gene's ear, words that Gene didn't understand. He felt himself grow cold as he heard them.

"Okay, okay. Stop it! But how...?" asked the dybbuk.

"I learned a lot from my father. Remember, I come from a long line of kabbalists."

"All right," said Jim quietly, trying to pull away from Aaron's tight grip around his body. "I'll go. But do it to me just once more, okay? Make me see the light and I'll let go of him forever. Do it like you did the last time we were here? Remember? It was almost too much but I wanted it so badly. Once more and I'll go and never come back."

"Promise?" asked Aaron, certain that a dybbuk could not lie when asked a direct question, only try to evade it.

"Yes, I promise."

They kissed.

An hour later Aaron was letting the first lashes fall on Jim's body. The moans that came from Jim's mouth, though, were unmistakably Gene's. Aaron's glove hand stroked the welts that rose on Jim's flesh, whispered encouragement into Jim's ear, all the time knowing that it was Gene who was the recipient of his efforts. The flogging reached a crescendo then waned, crescendoed again, each time sending Jim/Gene writhing against the restraints that sustained him. Aaron moved cautiously to each new peak at first, knowing that Gene could handle the intensity of the pain but not so sure Jim would be able to withstand it when he recovered his body.

Eventually Aaron heard Gene/Jim murmur, "Almost there, almost..."

Aaron increased the rapidity of the strokes, let them fall where the flesh was already torn and bleeding, following his own instincts as he had with Gene so many times before. Letting himself go, as he knew he must, Aaron knew without being told that Gene/Jim was there, at the peak, finding the center within himself.

Suddenly Gene/Jim threw his head back and howled, "The light, Aaron! The light!"

Aaron let fall a final stroke across Jim's back, watched the body slump forward. There was a momentary glimmer of Jim returning to the eyes before Aaron saw his lover pass out from the pain. He had Jim back.

Quickly he unshackled Jim's limp body and laid him carefully on a nearby cot. Carefully he applied ice, then salve to the wounds, murmuring endearments to Jim as he did, kissing the tender flesh with aching lips. Then he sat and watched Jim sleep.

Hours later Jim opened his eyes.

"What happened?" he whispered.

Aaron gently lifted Jim up and gave him a long drink of water.

"I tell you later. Rest and heal for now, baby. Daddy wants you all to himself."

Jim fell back to sleep.

———◠———

Jim shook his head not believing, but still believing, the words Aaron was saying.

"What's it called? A dybbuk? Gene did that to me?"

"You called him," explained Aaron. "You loved him too much, but not enough to let him move on to wherever he was heading next."

"What do I do now?"

"Nothing. But before we leave, let's visit the bridge again. But this time say a final good bye and don't look back when you walk away. That's when a dybbuk latches on to the living."

"But –."

"It explains everything, Jimbo. Either that or we're both crazy. Which will it be?"

"The dybbuk, I guess, but –"

"But nothing, baby. Now Daddy wants you for himself. He hasn't done you, yet, just Gene."

Their lips met. Aaron's tongue slid deep into Jim's throat. Jim felt whole again, owned and cared for by the man who had rescued him from madness or worse. When Aaron entered him, he felt himself expand to receive him, then tighten to hold Aaron's fat cock securely inside him – so tight, he hoped, that Aaron's body would always be locked to his.

He felt safe now and wanted the feeling to last forever. Aaron fucked him as Jim knew he would, with passion and control, moving his pole inside Jim, first hitting one tender center and then another, finding all the secret spots that sent Jim into a frenzy of need and desire. Aaron fucked him harder, slapped him across the ass and then the face, then held him in a lip lock as he raced to finish inside him. Jim felt his own seed spill across his belly as Aaron made his final thrusts deep inside Jim's bowels. They called their joy in unison.

"Now," whispered Aaron, his voice hoarse from exertion. "You're mine, all mine."

"Yes, Sir."

"You must be mine."

"Yes, Daddy."

"Mine because I love you..."

Together, their bodies sticky with sweat and cum, they drifted off to sleep, Aaron's cock still inside Jim. As he fell asleep, Jim fingered the chain collar locked around his neck and sighed, content.

Before they left they stopped at the bridge over the Keizersgracht. Aaron said something in Hebrew, a blessing Jim supposed. Jim stood looking over the water and said quietly, but loud enough for Aaron to hear, "Bye, buddy. It's been great but it's over now. You move on to wherever and I'll see there soon enough. But not before. For now, Gene, so long."

They walked away from the canal, away from the Homomonument and Gene's watery grave, hand in hand. Heading down Raadhuissstraat, they discussed where to have dinner on this, their last night in Amsterdam. Neither looked back.

Dybbuk: **Yiddish. The soul of a dead individual that inhabits the body of a living person, sometimes taking over his or her life.**

ABOUT THE AUTHOR

Starting out in life as a nice boy from a good family looking desperately for the wrong crowd, David May started writing as a child. After graduating from UC Santa Cruz, he moved to San Francisco where he initially gained notoriety in 1984 when his first story, **Cutting Threads**, which was published in *Drummer,* sparking both controversy and praise from readers. A regular contributor to *Drummer* until its demise, May's work has also appeared in *Honcho, Mach, Advocate Men, Unzipped, Inches, Frontiers, Lambda Book Report, Harvard Gay & Lesbian Review, Cat Fancy, International Leatherman* and *Manifest Review.* David May's work, both fiction and nonfiction, can also be found in *Kosher Meat, Best of Gay Erotica 2003, Best of Gay Erotica 2007, Afterwords: Real Sex From Gay Men's Diaries, Bar Stories, Queer View Mirror, Flesh and the Word 3, The Mammoth Book of New Gay Erotica, Bears* and many other anthologies. In 2002 he moved to Seattle where he lives with, and is owned by, his Sir and two cats.

www.ingramcontent.com/pod-product-compliance
Lightning Source LLC
Chambersburg PA
CBHW071210260626
47162CB00004B/1250